I0626571

Billionaire Boys Club

J.L. Ryan

Published by J.L. Ryan, 2018.

This is a work of fiction. Similarities to real people, places, or events are entirely coincidental.

BILLIONAIRE BOYS CLUB

First edition. June 22, 2018.

Copyright © 2018 J.L. Ryan.

ISBN: 978-1393232964

Written by J.L. Ryan.

The Billionaire's Offer

Marisa stared down at the eviction notice, reading it a second time as her eyes skimmed over the letter. "You are hereby ordered to leave the premises in one week," she read out loud. She could feel the tears stinging the back of her eyes.

She knew that it was only a matter of time, being two months behind rent and no sign of when she could catch up, she was just thankful that they waited this long. She put the letter in her purse and got out of the car. She could only hope that hours at her waitress job would begin to pick up.

She entered the restaurant, passing through the dining area to get to the time clock. She nodded to the occasional regular customer, giving them her best smile. She didn't want to show the outside world just how much she was struggling.

When she got in the break room, she headed to the table that always held the new schedule. She looked around and saw that her friend, Chad, was there. "Hey, Marisa, the schedule isn't out yet."

"Oh..." her face fell, then went to the hallway where her boss' door was wide open. "Is Frank in a good mood?" she asked, with a lighthearted laugh.

Chad shrugged, "Haven't really had to talk to him." He stood up from the table and smiled her way. "See ya around."

She nodded, "Bye, Chad."

She headed down the hallway and peeked inside to find that he was looking down at some papers and she wondered if it was the schedule. She knocked and he looked up briefly, then his head went back down. "Hello," he mumbled.

"Hello," she nervously looked around the office. "May I talk to you for just a minute?"

He seemed to groan, as he looked back up. "Sure."

"Well...I don't exactly know how to approach the subject."

He rolled his eyes, "Just say it."

She sat down in the chair that was facing him. His expectant stare was nerve wracking. "See, I was hoping that maybe next week I could have some extra hours, anything that you can give me." She was pleading, but she was desperate. She didn't want to tell him about the eviction notice, so she hoped that it wouldn't come to that."

He looked away from her. She saw a pained expression in his eyes. "Marisa, we need to talk." She didn't like the sound of that, but she just nodded. "I was going to tell everyone this in a couple of days, but there really is no reason dragging it on. You have been a valuable employee for the last five years and I owe you that much."

Her jaw dropped, it didn't sound like happy news that he was about to share. "What are you trying to say, Frank?"

His eyes feel to the stack of papers on his desk. He leaned forward, ruffling through the stack. When his hand landed on a paper, he removed it and handed it to her. She looked down at the pink slip. She skimmed through the notice stating that she was being fired. She looked up at him, but couldn't find the words. "I'm sorry, Marisa. If I had any other way...I would take it."

"You're firing me?"

"I'm closing the restaurant," he slowly spoke. "It hasn't been good for us. You know the lack of hours and I don't foresee it getting better."

"When?" she asked, hoping that the tears wouldn't start falling.

"The buyer wants us out in two weeks."

She covered her face. She was at a loss for words. "So, you have already sold it?"

He nodded, "I didn't want to spring it on you guys."

She stood up from the chair, angry that her world was spinning out of control. She couldn't fight back the tears much longer. "Spring it on us? Frank, we all have to look for jobs. Did you think of that?"

"I know, but..."

She brushed away a tear that had fallen down her cheek. "I'm sorry, but you don't know." She looked away, "I have to clock in." She turned from him.

"Marisa, wait..." he began.

She just shook her head and glanced back toward him. "I need time to think."

"Please don't tell anyone."

She turned around and sighed heavily. "Really? You want the rest of the staff to be shocked by the news more than they already will be?"

"I need to tell them and I will tell them."

She nodded, "Fine. I'll give you twenty four hours," she headed out of the office and slid her badge through the time clock. She let out a slow breath, to calm down her nerves, before pushing through the break room door. She needed to figure out what she was going to do and she had no time to waste.

***

Marisa walked in her apartment and headed for the kitchen. She reached for the bottle of wine to pour herself a glass. She needed something to unwind with. When she poured the glass and lifted it to her lips, she found herself thinking about what she was going to do. She put the glass down and left the kitchen.

She went to her room and grabbed her laptop and then took it back to the kitchen. She took a drink and then turned the computer on.

She punched in a website to search for a job. As she narrowed it down to places that were based on location, she gradually looked down the list. She sipped her wine, taking in the positions. Many of the places she wasn't qualified for, but then her eyes fell on a few positions that were in search of secretaries, assistants, or receptionists.

She jotted down their information, then closed her laptop. She figured it was too late to do anything about the eviction, but she needed to find a job. She downed the rest of the wine and put the dish in the sink.

She headed upstairs and turned on the water in the bath, pouring in his some bubbles. She pulled her clothes off and got into the bath, sinking down so that the bubbles were covering her completely. She could feel the tears falling down her face and she sniffled.

She hated feeling this way. She was alone and losing everything that was important to her. As she wiped a tear from her eye, she heard her cellphone ringing. She grabbed a towel, wiping her arms off and then reached across to her pants, where she removed the phone. She saw on the caller ID that it was her mother. She groaned, but quickly answered the call. "Hey, Mom."

"How's it going?" She asked. Her voice was cheerful, causing Marisa to try to push away her worries.

"Oh...same ol' same ol'," she lied. "How have you guys been?"

"We have been good. We were hoping you would come home for the Independence Day Barbeque this year."

When she was living at home, she loved the barbeque. However, she was now twenty-five and had moved away nearly seven years ago. She only went home for the occasional Christmas when she didn't have to work. "I think I'll have to work that day and won't be able to come back." Again, she stated a lie.

There was a long pause on the other end, before her mother spoke up. "Please try. Your sister has some news and we would love to see you."

News? Marisa thought. "I'll see what I can do. I have two weeks to see if I can work it out."

"So, you are going to try?" Her mother sounded hopeful.

"I said I would, but I can't make any promises," she snapped, then felt bad that it came across that way. "I'm sorry Mom. It's just things have been busy."

"I understand," her mother replied and Marisa knew that she really had no idea. "We just really miss you."

"Yes, I know. I miss you guys, too." When she lived at home, her best friend was her sister, who just happened to be only five years younger than her. It was tough on all of them when she decided to take off right out of high school. "Hey, I better go. I hear the doorbell." She spoke, just wanting to get off the phone.

"Goodbye, Mom."

"Goodbye, Honey. I'll talk to you soon."

"Okay," she quickly hung up the call and pushed her phone away from her. She didn't have time to worry about her parents, too. She sighed, closing her eyes. She prayed that she would find a job quickly and all of this could be put behind her.

She unplugged the bath and stepped out of the tub. She would get some much needed rest and then spend all day job searching, if necessary, until she had the perfect one.

***

She crossed off the second job on her list and glanced over the openings. She wasn't having the best luck, but she still had several positions open that she could apply for. She drove a few blocks and turned a corner, where a large law office stood in front of her. She parked the car and crossed her fingers, heading up to the door.

When she entered, she looked around until she saw a wall that had several names on it. She walked over and glanced down at the listing. "Martz, Tucker, and Bradley Law Firm," she whispered and then glanced up at the wall and noticed the name in gold letters.

She headed in the direction the arrow pointed, to where she was brought to a narrow hallway.

She saw the glass door with the name of the law firm and she went inside. She looked around to find a lot of bustling going on and people on the phone, talking over copy machines. She noticed a blonde woman, staring at her computer, but she didn't seem too distracted by other things going on. So, she approached her.

When she didn't look up, she cleared her throat. Finally the woman looked up, clearly annoyed. "May I help you?" She snapped.

"Uh..." Marisa looked down at her chicken scratch on the notepad. "I am interested in applying for the job."

The woman rolled her eyes, "You and every other teeny bopper."

"I'm not teeny bopper. I'm twenty-five and..." she began, but that made the woman appear even more annoyed.

"Yeah, did I ask?" She replied, rolling her eyes.

Marisa felt awkward in that moment, nearly stepping back, apologizing for wasting her time, and leaving. "Um, I—"

"Go through that door," she interrupted, "until you will find a large desk and you can ask about the position there. This is a mail room only and we don't handle such things. If you would have come through the other door, you would have clearly noticed that." She laughed with sarcasm and then went back to her work.

Marisa wanted to say, *did I ask?* However, she refrained from being sarcastic and headed toward the door. She opened the door to find a much more reserved area. She walked up to the desk and a middle-aged redhead looked up and smiled. "Hello, may I help you?"

"Yes, I would like to apply for the position that I saw online."

The girl nodded, "Of course. The way interviews are being handled is by being interviewed on the spot. It usually lasts about a half an hour. Are you free to stay?"

Marisa's eyes got big and she nodded, "Of course."

"Great. I will see if the boss is available. Please, have a seat over there," she pointed to the chairs and Marisa went and took a seat. She found herself extremely nervous, as she scrunched the paper in her hands and waited for a response. It was about five minutes later, when she was walking back to her. "You may follow me."

Marisa attempted several short breaths, to gain her composure. When they reached a door, she noted that she was still as nervous as ever. The woman opened the door, allowing her to walk into an office.

The moment she got inside, she saw a tall, dark, and gorgeous guy sitting at his computer.

Her voice escaped her, as he looked up. He had the most magnetizing blue eyes, with brown wavy hair. His smile was charismatic and she was completely gone. "Hello. Please have a seat." He motioned to the chair in front of his desk.

She sat down, unable to function while looking at him. He smiled, cocking an eyebrow and giving her a peculiar look. "Why don't you start off with something about yourself."

She searched for the words, realizing that she had to say something. "Um...my...my name is Marisa Jamison."

"Ms. Jamison, it is a pleasure meeting you." Again he smiled and she was caught off guard. "My name is Jeffrey Bradley, one of the lawyers here." She smiled, still unable to speak. "Why don't you tell me about your experience."

She looked down at her hands, then slowly her eyes went back to him. "Well, I don't really have much experience. I currently work at a restaurant."

"For how long?" He asked, taking down notes.

"Five years," she replied, hoping to soon start breathing regularly again.

"It is true that this is different from a restaurant, but you have to have customer service skills."

"I definitely have that," she spoke, suddenly feeling a bit better.

He smiled, "Tell me why you would want to work in a place like this?"

"Well, the restaurant I work in is getting ready to close and a lot of positions that I was looking at require more experience. I think this would be an interesting job." She shrugged, "I am a quick learner."

He took down some more notes and then looked up. "Well, there have been several applicants. Some more qualified than others. The pay is competitive and we offer a strong benefits package. You would start at $55,000 a year."

She nearly fell off her chair. "Are...are you serious?"

He nodded, "Did I stutter?" His face was blank, like he had flipped a switch and joined the dark side, but then quietly laughed and she shook off the strange feeling she had.

"No, but just a bit taken aback."

He nodded, regaining his smile. He then stood up and she figured that the interview was over. She was bummed to realize that it was only about fifteen minutes and she figured that that was not a good sign. She stood up and shook his outstretched hand. "When can you start?"

Her jaw dropped, "I'm sorry?"

He shot another glare in her direction. "When....can...you...start? My assistant quit last minute and I need a replacement." He stated, slowly easing out the words.

"As soon as you need me." She conceded, knowing that she would have to work around her work schedule. She just was elated by the turn of events.

"Okay, then I will see you tomorrow." He sat down and went back to his computer.

She processed the words in her mind, but before leaving she glanced back in his direction. "Tomorrow is Saturday."

He nodded, "I'm aware, Ms. Jamison." She paused at his door, but he looked up. "Is working a Saturday not a possibility for you?"

She was worried that he would snatch the job away, so she quickly shook her head. "No, Saturday is great. Thank you!" She left his office and silently celebrated that things were looking up. Tomorrow was a new day and she wouldn't focus on everything she lost, but everything she was gaining.

***

It wasn't until she was home and in bed that she even thought about how she didn't know what time she should be there. She decided to just go in at eight o'clock and hope that that was fine with him. She dressed in her dressier clothes and headed to the office.

When she got there, there was another car in the parking lot. She parked and went up to the door. As she walked through the offices, she noticed that the once bustling of a mailroom, was deafly quiet. She glanced around the room and then went to the other part of the office.

She opened the door to find that it was also quiet. She casually walked down the hallway, the only sound was the clicking of her black high heels. She went to his door and saw him through the glass door, busy at his computer. She knocked softly. "Come in!" He called. She entered, but he didn't bother looking up. "You're late," he mumbled, continuing to type away.

"I...I'm really sorry. We didn't really..."

He put up his hand and looked at her, "Don't let it happen again."

"Yes, sir," she mumbled.

He stood up and walked around the desk, glancing over her outfit and causing her to feel awkward. "You also don't have to be so dressed up, unless we have a meeting." She glanced down at her outfit and frowned, but didn't say anything.

"Follow me," he ordered. They left the office and headed back down the hallway. He pushed a door open and they entered, bringing her into another office. "This is your office. You can decorate as you please, but don't get too caught up in it. You will do a lot of work in my office and be expected to do whatever I ask of you." He hesitated, a heated stare appeared. "Whatever I ask you. Understand?"

She took a step back from him. She felt a strange sensation as he spoke to her. It was like he was cutting to her core and she couldn't understand what was happening. "Yes, I understand," she spoke, but she wasn't sure if she really did.

"Perfect." He leaned over the phone and pressed a button. "When you need to talk to me, press this button. It will buzz and inform me that you are calling me.

When I call you, you will hear a buzz and you answer by pressing this button." He looked at her, shifting to stare into her eyes. "Do you need to take notes?"

She nearly laughed, then shook her head. "I think I have it, but thanks."

She couldn't help but notice how his demeanor was different from the interview. He was belittling and acting like he was better than her. She felt like a child he was training to ride a bike or use the restroom.

It was a different phase that she wasn't expecting. "Suit yourself." He shrugged, heading out the door. "Get comfortable with the office and I will get with you soon."

"Thank you," she mumbled, walking around the desk and sinking down in the chair. She felt out of her element and hoped that it was just nerves, because she was already hooked into the job.

The money would be more than enough to keep herself in the apartment. She started messing with the computer, getting a feel of the drawers in her desk, and swiveling in her chair, when she heard the phone buzzing at her.

She stopped what she was doing and stared at the phone. She pressed the button that he showed her. "Y...yes?"

"Jamison, come to my office," he ordered. His voice was almost gruff.

"Yes..." she started to say, but she heard a tone that signified he was no longer on the intercom.

She rolled her eyes and headed back to his office.

She went into his office and put on a smile. He stood up, with a pile of papers in his hand. He walked around and handed her the papers. She looked them over. "Follow me," he ordered.

She willingly did so, as he led her to another room. "Am I going to remember where everything is?" she asked, laughing lightly.

He turned around and his gaze was cold and distant. "Do I need to draw you a map?" He asked, with no sign of teasing. She shook her head and he turned back to the filing cabinets. "You are to file these forms by date that they were completed." He pointed to the date and then looked up at her, "Understand?"

She nodded. "Good!" He mumbled, heading out of the room and leaving her alone. She frowned, turning back to the filing cabinet. She didn't know why he had to be such a jerk, but she wasn't going to jeopardize it by questioning his actions. He was the boss and that was what she would keep telling herself, because it was going to pay the bills and that was what mattered most.

***

Marisa woke up to the knock on her apartment door. She glanced at the clock and frowned, "Six o'clock?" She mumbled, putting on her robe and stumbling to the door. The knock happened again. "Coming!" she called, hoping it didn't across as gruff. She opened the door to see that Jeffrey Bradley was at her door.

She quickly pulled the strap tighter around her robe. She was not used to awkwardly standing in front of her boss, wearing just a nightie and a robe. "What are you doing here?" She asked, realizing how rude it came across. She didn't care; she figured that it still wasn't as rude as he had been the past three days.

"I told you we had meetings today." He brushed into the apartment. When she turned around, she saw that his eyes were casually washing over her body. "Are you going to be dressed like that for every meeting we have?"

She looked down at her outfit and then glared at him. "Smart..." she finally said. "If I would have known that you were going to be here at the early light of dawn, I would have been sure to put on a formal gown."

For the first time, since he hired her, she noticed a smile on his face. She had to take a step back, because she didn't expect for a simple smile to melt her heart. "I apologize. You are most correct. I didn't tell you about the fact that I like to prepare for the meetings. Since the first one is at eight o'clock, I was just trying to get a head start. I can come back."

As he was passing her, she reached out and grabbed his arm. He turned to look at her and she shrugged, "You're here now...you might as well make the best of the time. Have a seat at the kitchen table and I will hurry and take a shower, get dressed, and be back before you know it."

"If you insist."

She rolled her eyes. She didn't really feel like she had much choice. "I do." She left him standing there and hurried into her bedroom, where she grabbed a change of clothes and then went into the bathroom. She would make it a quick shower and then be out there and ready to start the day.

She barely had time to think, before she was turning the shower off and getting dressed. She threw her hair back in a ponytail and went out to the kitchen.

He looked up, "That didn't take long," he muttered.

"Told you I would be fast," She replied, sitting down across from him.

"Indeed you did," he replied, pushing the paperwork in front of her. "We are meeting with Troy Houser. He is suing his ex for full custody of his two children."

"That seems harsh," she mumbled.

"Excuse me?" He asked, looking intently at her.

"I just mean that she's their mother. Why would he do that?" She shook her head, leafing through the papers.

He opened another folder and pushed it toward her. She looked down to see a picture of a little girl, a bruise on her arm.

She looked up at him, "Is there proof that the mother did this?"

He shook his head, "No, but that's why I'm here...to find proof."

Marisa snickered, "Whatever makes you sleep at night." She put the folder down and closed it up.

"What do you mean by that?" He asked, clearly angered by her attitude.

"You may be looking for proof to prove something that isn't there. Maybe you are defending the wrong person. Ever think of that?"

"Why are you so convinced that he's in the wrong? You know nothing about this case."

"Maybe not, but I'm just saying that you shouldn't just believe him because he's your client." She spoke, crossing her arms and staring at him.

"Duly noted, Jamison, but I don't recall hiring you to be a lawyer. This is my case and my job is to prove that he is the better option for those two kids."

"Even if he's not?" She asked, calmly.

"It's the price a lawyer pays. You don't always get the innocent one." He pulled the papers back toward him and continued to leaf through the files. She watched him, but she felt a feeling of dread inside of her. She heard a knock at her door. Their eyes met, as she got up and went to the door.

She opened the door to find her landlord on her step. She glanced back to her boss and then pushed her way out the door. "What do you want, Harry?" She asked.

"Have you thought about that letter I gave you? You only have three days to make your move...either pay up or get out. What will it be?"

She could feel the tears at the back of her eyes, but she begged for them not to fall. "I know. I'm working on it."

"Friday...that's your last day. I don't want to lose you as a tenant, but I have a business to run."

He turned away and headed to the stairs, "Goodbye!" she mumbled.

She went back into her apartment and saw that he was watching the door. She didn't respond about the visitor, but he did speak. "Friend?" He asked, casually.

"More like enemy," she replied with a laugh. She shrugged, "Back to this case. I will step back and let you do your job."

"Thank you!" He removed a couple of pictures from the file and held them up. "We do have proof that she had been having an affair with this guy, while she was still married."

She nodded, *still doesn't make her an abuser,* she thought. She pushed the thought from her mind and reached out for the picture. She looked down and saw this woman dancing with this man. They looked like they were in love. She gave the picture back to him and shrugged. "Nice picture," she mumbled.

"For a cheater," he replied, shaking his head. "I guess that's it. I am sorry that I interrupted your morning."

"No worries."

"I'll see you in the office in about an hour."

She nodded, watching him leave her apartment. She sunk down at the kitchen table and covered her face with her hands. She didn't want him to know what was bothering her, so she had to hold it in. Yet, she had no idea what she was going to do.

***

Jeffrey buzzed in on her phone at eight o'clock sharp. "Yes?" She asked.

"The client is here. Come to my office first."

"Yes, Mr. Bradley," she spoke, picking up a pad of paper and pen and heading out of her office. She walked down the hallway and entered his office.

He looked up and then stood to his feet. "I just wanted to make sure we were on the same page about today's meeting."

"Meaning?" she asked.

"I don't want you speaking your mind. I get that you aren't convinced, but it's not my job to convince you. It's my job to convince the judge and I don't want you getting in that way." He moved to the door and held it open for her. "Understand?"

"Loudly," she spoke, brushing past him. She turned around and put up her finger. "For the record...I would never get in the way of YOU doing your job." She turned on her heels and walked down the hallway to the boardroom. She stopped and turned around to see that he was lagging behind.

He held out his hand to show that he was welcoming her in first. She nodded and entered the room. She smiled as she took a seat. "Hello, Mr. Houser," she shook his hand.

She saw that Jeffrey was doing the same, as he took his seat. He put the paperwork in front of him and then looked up. "Tell me your story, Mr. Houser."

She watched, as he seemed hesitant. However, then he finally spoke. "I am suing for full custody, because my wife isn't suitable."

"You mean your ex?" He asked.

He nodded, "Yeah...yeah, my ex. She isn't suitable. She drinks and has abusive tendencies."

Marisa jotted down the information, as he stated them. "Tell me about her a

busive tendencies."

"Well...when Valarie was two she ended up with a broken arm."

Marisa looked up at him and saw that he was sweating profusely. "Your ex beat her so bad that she broke her arm?" He asked, making notes of his own.

He nodded, but then paused. "They said that she fell off the Merry Go Round, but I never bought that. I know my ex."

"When did you get divorced? How old were the children?" Jeffrey asked.

"Hm..." he looked up to the ceiling. "I think that Valarie was four years old and Trey was two."

"So, you divorced her two years after the suspected abuse started?"

"Yes, so?" He asked, defensively. "I loved her and I didn't want to believe that she could be a maniac, but the truth had to come out."

"How old are the children now?" He asked, barely making eye contact.

"That was two years ago." He spoke, carefully looking between the two people sitting opposite him.

"So, it was about four years ago that Valarie broke her arm?" Marisa glanced at Jeffrey. She could tell where he was going with it, but she wondered if he was questioning him because of her or because of him.

"What does that matter?" Troy asked, again defensively.

"Nothing. I just want to see how you handle the questions that you are going to be fired. What I am asking is only the breaking point. If you don't answer them with ease, you'll be perceived as hiding something. Are you hiding something?"

Again I turned my focus on my boss. He was good and not batting an eye. For a moment it made sense why he was arrogant. It was the only way he knew how to be. "Nothing. She deserves to suffer, because those kids belong with me."

"Okay," Jeffrey replied, taking some more notes. "Do you have anything else to add?"

He shook his head, "Nope. I have said my peace." He replied.

For the first time since entering the room, Jeffrey turned to Marisa. She couldn't read what was in his mind, but she wondered if it was doubt. He stood up and turned back to Troy.

"Thank you for stopping by and I will let you know when you go before the judge." They all shook hands again and Troy left the room.

Jeffrey followed after him, not saying a word to Marisa as he headed back to his office. Marisa looked down at her notes and noticed what she had written. Most of it was about his attributes. He was shaking, nervous, sweating, and defensive. He didn't act like something that believed what he was saying and somehow she wanted to prove that.

***

Marisa sat at her desk, tapping her pencil loudly against her computer. Her thoughts roamed to the landlord and the meeting with their client. She finally took a deep breath and headed out of her office. She made her way down to see him. She noticed the door was open, but she knocked anyway. He looked up,

"Come in, Jamison." There was something about the way that he called her by her last name. She loved it. His eyes remained on hers. "Well, are you going to stand all day gawking, or do you have a question?"

She felt her face flush, as she looked away. She didn't know how he could do that. When she finally regained control, she looked back in his direction. "What did you think of the meeting?" She asked. It wasn't exactly why she came in there, but she figured it would buy her some time.

He shrugged, "Okay, I guess. Why? I suppose you have an opinion." He snarled.

She shrugged, "Maybe, but I won't say a word. I'm a woman of my word."

He laughed, glancing down at the papers. "Well, if you do decide to voice your opinion...I'll listen." She was surprised to hear him say that. He looked up and she thought she even noticed a smile. "Doesn't mean I'll take your side. It just means I'll listen."

"Right," she shook her head. She glanced down at the picture on his desk. For the first time, really noticing it. "Is that your family?" She asked, staring at a picture of a brunette woman, holding a toddler in her hands. His hand was on her shoulder.

She glanced at his hand and noticed that he wasn't wearing a wedding ring. She had figured she would have seen it before, if he had been.

He nodded, "Yes," he replied, but the word came out quiet.

"Good looking family," she replied, then turned to leave, but when she reached the door she decided to just say what was on her mind. "I guess I do have something to ask you."

He looked up, "About the case?"

"Well...not exactly."

He put down his papers and nodded, "Go on."

She felt panic welling up inside of her. She then tried to breathe and think of how she could possibly approach the subject with someone that she barely knew. "You see...I was kind of hoping that possibly you could give me an advance on my first paycheck?"

If there was once a smile playing on his face, it was now gone. "I don't do charity." He replied, looking down at the papers.

Her jaw dropped, "Charity?"

"Yes. I believe in working your way from the bottom and knowing that it will all work out in the end. I don't give handouts."

She couldn't believe her ears. She believed that you should fight to get ahead, but she also believed in doing something for the good of the cause. Yet, this had nothing to do with charity.

"It would ultimately be my money. I'm not understanding the problem." She replied, feeling a sense of urgency.

He rolled his eyes, "Yes, but if I do it for you this one time then you are going to expect every time. That's the way things work."

"You're wrong. I just need some extra money this week. I didn't make a lot at the waitressing job and things got behind. I really could just use a jumpstart."

He shook his head, glancing down at his desk. "I can't do that. You may see yourself out."

She felt her face turning red, but this time in anger. "You know what you are?" She fired out.

He looked up, eyes wide, "No...what am I?"

She stared him down, bracing herself and trying to hold it all in, but it was impossible. "You are an arrogant jerk that doesn't care about anyone or anything. All you want to do...is be right.

Well, newsflash...you aren't right. You are conceited and if it wasn't for the fact that I need this job, I would...I would..."

He stood up from his desk, "You would what?"

"I would quit, because I didn't apply to be a doormat or a slave and in the few days I have worked with you...that is exactly what I am."

"Are you finished?" He asked, when she took time to breathe. She nodded. "For the way you just talked to me, I could have you fired and you wouldn't have to worry about quitting."

She looked away. At that point she didn't think her life could get worse anyway. "I will willingly go," she mumbled.

She reached the door, but he cleared his throat. "Don't go...I'm not through talking." She casually looked up at him, waiting for him to continue. "I could easily let you go and not turn back, but I'm not going to."

Her jaw dropped, "You're not?"

He shook his head, "No. In fact, I appreciate when someone can speak their mind and not back down. Not everyone does that and it's a trait that I admire."

She was not the least bit surprised to learn that. She felt a twinge of hope. "So, you'll give me the advance?"

Their eyes met, but he finally shook his head. "I can't. I know that you think that I'm a hard-nose and maybe you're right, but the fact is that companies have rules for a reason and one of the rules that I stand by is you need to work for everything you receive. It may seem tough, but it seems to always work."

She groaned, nodding her understanding. "Then, I guess it is what it is. Thank you for your time."

"Unless you would like to tell me what you want the money for and perhaps we could work out a loan agreement."

She paused at the door. Every thought she was hearing was telling her to swallow her pride and just tell him, but she sadly felt she couldn't. She felt like a failure and she didn't want him judging her. "Not that important," she said and then walked out of his office. She headed back to her office and sat down at her desk. She was thankful she still had a job, but the realization that she was about to lose her home...was a tough pill to swallow.

***

Jeffrey sunk back in his oversized desk chair. His eyes fell to the picture of his family. He picked it up and looked at it, running his fingers over the picture of his daughter. "He closed his eyes," I love you, Jasmine." He replaced the picture and went back to his work.

His mind drifted away to the feisty blonde. He saw the pain in her eyes and part of him considered just giving her the advance, but he was a stubborn man and not too proud to admit that.

He looked at his notes that he had taken on Troy Houser and began reading them out loud, "Nervous, edgy, argumentative, anxious..." each thing he wrote down was a trait that he saw coming from his client. He didn't know why, but he suddenly had a strange feeling about the whole situation.

He thought back to Marisa's doubts at the very beginning, but then shook off the nagging feeling that he was getting. "I have to trust him," he whispered, putting the notes away.

He stood up and moved to his sports jacket. He headed out of his office. On the way out of the building, he passed her office.

He looked inside to see that she was still at her desk, tapping her pencil on the computer and staring aimlessly at the screen. He wondered what was so interesting. "Are you leaving?" He asked.

She looked up, shrugging. "Why? Do you have a time that I have to be out of the office if you're not here?" She asked, sarcastically.

The way she was aggressive toward him, he noticed how it affected him. He had never seen anything like it. Jordan had left the job because she wasn't able to keep up with his sarcastic antics, but he could see that he was meeting his match. "No...no curfew." He tapped the wall and nodded, "Have a good evening."

He heard her snickering, as he left the office. He knew that there was something she was hiding and he hoped to be the one to crack her code. He smiled, walking out of the building. It would be fun trying.

***

She grabbed her last box and headed out of her apartment. "Thanks for helping me move, Chad. I didn't know who else to call."

He shrugged, "What about your new boss?"

She thought about that and rolled her eyes. "I doubt Mr. Bradley would be the moving kind of man. Besides..." her face fell, "I don't want him to know where I'm staying."

"I wish you would change your mind, Marisa." He spoke, while putting the boxes in the back of his truck. "I have plenty of room."

She knew that it was a generous offer, but she couldn't take him up on that. "I appreciate it, Chad, but I'll be fine. This is only until I start getting regular checks."

They got into his truck and as he pulled away, she turned to him, "Have you decided what you're going to do when the restaurant is closed?"

"Probably collect unemployment until I find something else." He shrugged, "Not really worried about it."

"I miss everyone," she replied, quietly.

He turned and looked at her, when they stopped at a red light. "Everyone misses you, too."

She knew part of her reasons of missing them, was the fact that Jeffrey Bradley just wasn't them. He turned into the hotel that was next to the office. They got out and grabbed her few boxes. They walked into the lobby and she went up to the reception desk. She hoped that they could strike up a deal and not charge her the whole fee up front. She explained the situation and was relieved when they agreed to bill her at the end of each week.

"Thank you!" she replied, gratefully.

She turned to Chad and they walked to the elevator. "You have one more chance to change your mind. A hotel is not a place for someone to live."

She laughed, "I will be fine. At least I'm close to the office." They reached the floor and she got off, walking to the door. She opened the door and entered the room. It wasn't big, but she could make it work. They put the boxes down and she walked to the window.

She peered outside and she laughed, "I even have a view of the office...what more could I ask for?"

He laughed, walking over to look outside. "Not bad," he spoke, but sounding a tad sarcastic. "I'll call you later and we'll go out. You could use a night out."

"You'll have to use my number here. I got rid of my cellphone."

"Okay," she walked over and wrote down the number on a piece of paper. She handed it to him and he put it in his pocket. "Take care, Marisa."

"You, too." She pulled him into a hug. "Thank you for helping pack."

"When you move out of here, I'll be back."

She smiled, nodding. "I will keep that in mind."

He headed to the door and they said their goodbyes. When he was gone, she looked out the window. She noticed that the office building was opening and Jeffrey was leaving. She glanced down at the clock to find that it was seven o'clock on a Friday night and he was just now leaving. She shook her head.

She wondered if his wife ever questioned his later nights. She closed the blinds and fell back against her bed, plopping down on the comforter. Her eyes closed and she drifted off to sleep, not wasting any time.

***

The next morning, she arrived to work on another Saturday. She didn't anticipate having to work the extra weekends at a job that clearly stood for Monday to Friday. However, she kept thinking about the salary and it suddenly became alright.

She hurried into the office, this time beating him. She put her stuff away and logged into her computer. She was busy looking up the information about various prospective clients that he asked her to research, when she saw him looking in her office. "Good Morning!"

He cocked his head, "You're here early."

"I wanted to get working on the research. Is that a crime?" She asked.

She had quickly discovered the best way to get to him, was by acting like him. While she didn't like to perceive herself as rude and arrogant, she would do anything stand up to him.

"Not at all, I'm impressed," he admitted.

She looked up, as he was walking out of her office. She was confused by some of his attitude shifts. She went back to looking up the research. She jotted down notes of things that he might find beneficial.

When she was done with his list, she got up and went to his office. She put the packet down on his desk and turned away. "Wait a minute, Marisa."

She turned around, "You need me to do something else?" She asked.

He looked through her notes and placed them on his desk. Their eyes met and he shifted in his seat. "Is everything alright? Something seems different."

"Everything's fine," she spoke. "Anything else?"

He shook his head, "I don't mean to be abrasive...at least not all the times," he laughed, but she didn't crack a smile. "You just seem to be a little upset about something." He paused, "If this is about the advance, maybe I was a little stern. You don't get paid for another week and I suppose I could get you part of your first paycheck." He pulled out his checkbook and she stared at him. He appeared to be using his own personal checks. "Would five hundred cover it?"

"Mr. Bradley, forget about it." She looked away, but he remained with his pen poised.

"No, I'm prepared to do this." He argued.

She didn't understand the sudden change. "That's nice, but you might as well give it up. The reason I requested the advance is no longer prevalent. Thank you, though."

She turned away and headed out of the office. She didn't want him to see her flustered, but she felt dizzy. She went back in her office and sat down. She nervously began drumming her fingers on her desk.

She tried to get focused on the next tasks on her list, but she was still struggling at his immense change of heart. It didn't add up. She began typing on her computer and getting her mind on other projects, that she didn't realize how late it had become. She heard the buzzing of her phone. She looked down at the phone, like it had grown a head.

She pushed the button, "H...hello?"

"Jamison, will you please come into my office?"

Please? She thought. "Yes, sir." She replied, getting up and heading back to the office. She glanced at her watch and saw that it was past lunchtime.

She knocked on his closed door. "Come in!" His voice wasn't gruff, but instead inviting.

She opened the door and hesitated, before pushing through the door. When he looked up, it was definitely a smile on his face. "Yes?"

He stood up and moved closer to her, "I just wanted to invite you out for lunch. You have been working so hard and I thought we could both use a break."

She fought the urge to check his forehead to see if he was running a fever. "Well, I was planning on just going home."

"Home? That's several blocks away. This way you can get something to eat right away and it's my treat. What do you say?" She hesitated, but finally nodded. "Good," he spoke and it came out enthusiastically. He grabbed his sports jacket and followed her out the door. She stopped at her office and grabbed her purse and then they were off. She was confused, but she was hungry and figured that it wouldn't hurt to just go out for a bite to eat. At least she hoped not.

***

He waited for her to place her order and then he placed his. The waiter left and he turned to her. He didn't know why he was suddenly nervous. He didn't remember ever feeling this way about a woman or anyone else. "So, tell me about you Marisa." He replied, taking a drink of his coffee.

"Marisa?" She asked. Her face turned red. "I don't think you have ever called me that."

"That's your name, isn't it?"

She laughed. "Yes, but I didn't think you knew that. You usually call me Jamison."

He hadn't really thought about that, but he knew that his way of keeping distance between him and someone was to call them by their last name. "Which do you prefer?" He asked, feeling his throat getting dry.

She seemed to contemplate that, "Either."

He smiled, "So, whatever I'm in the mood for?"

"Something like that," she replied with a chuckle. He hadn't noticed her laugh before, but it filled a room and he was drawn to it. There was a long pause, before she spoke. "There's something that I have been wanting to ask you. It's just something that I was interested in."

He took another drink, preparing himself. "Okay. What's that?"

"Well, at the interview I was told that there were several applicants. Yet, you hired me right away. Why?"

He hadn't expected her to be so bold to ask the question. Yet, he really didn't expect her to be so bold about anything. He was wrong about that. "I suppose there was something about you that I felt would be the perfect match to the job."

"That seems vague," she replied laughing.

"Yeah, I suppose it is. It's like when you go out looking for a pair of shoes and you know the exact style you're looking for. You just know and there's no point in waiting for another pair of shoes to come along, when you have the perfect pair right in front of you. Make sense?" He asked.

"Yes, you're comparing me to shoes."

He laughed, this time feeling a blush brushing across his face. "It's just an analogy. When you walked through the door...I just knew."

He hoped it didn't come across as corny, but he knew that it was the truth. By the look on her face, it definitely appeared that she was not thinking it was corny. "Okay, then if that's how you feel...why have things been tense between us?"

The food came and he paused, giving him time to think. When the waiter was gone, he looked back in her direction. "They say opposites attract, so it's obvious you and I would repel. We're a lot alike." She opened her mouth, but he placed his hand up, halting her.

"I know you think that I'm arrogant and rude and any other name in the book. You have been very vocal about that, but I speak my mind and so do you. We are bound to butt heads, but that doesn't mean that at the end of the day I'm not thankful you walked through my door."

He realized the way that came out, but he wasn't about to apologize for it. "I think that we could in essence make a great team, because even though you don't see it...I do value your opinion."

"That makes me feel good. Thank you!"

He smiled, "Now, let's enjoy the food." He took a bite of his salad and saw that she was finally getting comfortable and he breathed a sigh of relief. Everything he had said to her was the truth. None of it was lines that he was just feeding her and he hoped that she understood that.

***

Marisa stared down at the picture of Troy's ex dancing with the other man. Her mind kept going back to lunch with Jeffrey. He definitely surprised her by the easy tone. She had expected everything to be awkward and then when he told her why he chose her for the job, she found herself distracted. There was a heat in his eyes when he spoke the words and she didn't know if it was because she was attracted to him or lonely, but she suddenly felt like doing more than going to lunch with him.

She shook her head, removing the vision from her mind. She looked back down at the picture, tracing the outline of the couple. As she was doing that, she picked up the picture and stared at an image that she hadn't seen before.

She got up and moved to the window light. In the corner there was a faint image of a man staring in the direction of the couple. It was definitely Troy. She was sure of it.

She got up and hurried to his office. She stopped when she heard his voice echoing through the door that was a crack. "You can't do this to me, Janelle. Haven't I lost enough?" She paused, leaning in toward his door. "Please, don't...Dammit..." she heard the sound of a slamming phone and she cautiously proceeded. She considered leaving, but she had come this far. She knocked and heard the faint sound of his voice, "Come in!"

She opened the door and saw that he was sitting at his desk, looking drugged. "I...I can leave," she stammered.

He shook his head, "Don't bother." He sat up in his chair. "Find something?"

She proceeded to his desk, awkwardly. She held the picture, but before putting it in front of him. "Tell me about you."

He looked up and confusion was evident. "Pardon me?"

She took the seat in front of me. "Well, it seems that I did most of the talking at lunch. I think you have a story to tell. What is it?"

He shook his head, "Not worth telling."

"Come on, Mr. Bradley. I'm sure there's something. You have a beautiful family. Start there."

When he looked up, she sat back. There was agony on his face and she regretted saying anything. He reached for the picture and stared at it. "Do you know why this picture is on my desk?"

She shook her head, "Probably because it's your family and you want to show them off."

"Well, at one time that was true. However, now it just holds bad memories." She watched as he traced the picture of his daughter. "Her name was Jasmine."

"Was?"

He nodded slowly, looking up. "She drowned last year. She was just five years old." He smiled, "Believe it or not, I used to be a very charismatic gentleman and a family man. However, one weekend we had decided to go camping and I was going to have to work late on Friday night.

So, I told them to go up without me and I would come up Saturday. My wife and daughter were in a boat when a storm came through. She tried everything she could, but the boat capsized and Jasmine went under. She was wearing a lifejacket, but the boat pinned her under.

My wife couldn't find her until it was too late." She could tell that the memories were painful and tears were forming on his eyes. "I never blamed her, but she didn't know how to swim and she blamed me for not being there."

"I'm so sorry, Mr. Bradley."

He nodded, "Please, call me Jeffrey." She nodded, as he continued. "She called me and I rushed to the hospital, but it was too late. Right after the funeral she said she wanted a divorce. It was an amicable one. We didn't have a prenuptial, but I didn't worry about her taking me to the cleaners. It finalized and I thought things were done.

My dad died last month." She covered her mouth, realizing the hurt he was feeling. "I was left a hefty sum of money. My ex is suing me for damages from the loss of her daughter."

"Can she do that?" She asked in disbelief.

He nodded, "Unfortunately, people sue for all types of reasons."

"It's your daughter, too." She argued.

"I know, but her heart is still healing." He frowned, "My heart is still healing."

"My feelings exactly." Marisa stated. She was irritated by the news, but she wanted him to know that she appreciated him telling her the story. "Thank you for opening up to me, but I just think that you're getting the raw end of the deal."

He smiled, "Yeah, you and me both." He shrugged, "It is what it is and I will just have to fight through. Justice will win out, right?"

"I suppose," she mumbled, staring down at the picture.

"You did want to show me something. What is it?" she got up and walked around his desk. She put the picture down in front of him and pointed out the image. She was so close to him, that she was sure her breath was tickling his skin.

Their eyes met and she saw a fury in his eyes. She looked down at the picture. "I think it's Troy."

He looked back to the picture and slowly nodded. "I'll be damned."

"If he was there and saw the affair happening before his eyes, he could have gotten jealous. There is just something about him that..."

"Doesn't feel right," he finished her sentence.

"You feel it, too?"

He nodded, "I just don't want to jump to conclusions, but this is a very good start." She stepped back from him, needing a breather. He stood up and turned to her, "Thank you for listening today and Monday we'll try to dig deeper into figuring out the truth." He moved closer to her and she thought she saw that his eyes moved to her lips briefly.

"I think I'm going to head for the day. You alright with that?"

He started to nod, but then his lips went down to hers and he kissed her. She pulled away, not knowing what she wanted. His eyes remained connected to hers. "I'm messed up, no good..." he started.

"I know...me too," she whispered.

However, that didn't stop the notion that she wanted to feel his body against hers. "Sexual encounters at work are never a good idea."

She nodded, "I know..." before she could get anything else out, she felt his hand snake around her neck and he was pulling her back into another kiss. "Hm..." she moaned. "Wait..." she breathlessly spoke, breaking from the passionate embrace. "Are we even thinking this over?"

He shook his head moving closer to her and putting his hands on her blouse. "We're being irrational. Just go for it. He ripped the shirt from her body and it fell to the floor. His lips went to her neck, while her hands went to his shirt, removing it from the confinement of his dress pants. She started off tediously undoing button after button, but then knew that she needed to move the show on the road. She busted open his shirt, the way that he had busted open hers. Her hands trailed down his chest, while he continued to kiss her neck. She arched her back, sighing against his kisses. His hands went behind her back, as he slowly removed her bra. Her breasts pressed hard against his bare chest.

Her hands went to his pants and she quickly removed them. They fell to the floor and he kicked them off. Then his hands went to his boxers and she drug them down his legs, while his hands tweaked her nipples. She eyed his erection, salivating at the sight. His hands slowly slid down her stomach and then wrapped around her back. He undid the zipper to her skirt and it fell to the floor. His hands went to her panties and he looped his fingers through them, tugging them off of her body. Before she had time to comprehend the next move, she felt him lifting her into his arms and laying her down on the floor. Their lips met, his tongue dipping inside her mouth. As their tongues clashed together, his hands continued to massage her breasts, gently feeling each part of her sensitive skin.

As he was just about to enter her, he pulled back. "I don't have a condom," he groaned, starting to regress.

She wrapped her arms around him and pulled him closer to her. "I'm on the pill," she whispered, as they kissed. "Ugh..." she groaned, arching her back, but not breaking from the kiss.

During each thrust, she was forced to part from the kiss. "Ugh...Oh God...yes..." she whimpered, barely able to get the words out, it felt so good. As one arm continued being wrapped around him, her other arm fell down to her side and she tried desperately to grab anything to hold onto, finally choosing for a leg to his chair. Her hips bucked against his.

He crashed against her, with a hunger that she never endured. "Oh God...yes...yes..." he cried, pressing harder to her core. "Ugh...ugh..." he groaned, digging deeper. She could feel him pulsating within her. "Damn..." he cried out.

"Ugh...ugh...yes...God yes..." she moaned, as her body seized. She sighed, unable to move, as his gyrations slowly began to come to an end. "Wow..." she sighed, closing her eyes and just lying there. As she was focusing on her next move, she felt hands on her legs, parting her ever so softly.

She didn't know what he was doing, because of her inability to see straight, but she felt the entrance his finger, as it dipped inside of her. She moaned, taking in his sensual moves. Then it was over and she was fighting disappointment, until she felt something else. She tried to control her breathing, as she felt his tongue exploring every inch of her body.

"Oh God..." she whispered, but bit back a guttural groan. He licked her all over and her eyes opened, staring at the ceiling of his office. She reached down and grabbed his head, holding him closer to her. "Yes..." she groaned, as he tenderly caressed her.

She felt the smoothness of his moves and she sighed against his deep and masculine movements. "Hm...hmmm...hm..." she signed, her body gliding against the intensity. As his tongue was seeking out each crevice that she could provide, she felt her body begin to shake with desire. "Oh God!" she cried. He licked her with satisfaction and not leaving anything behind.

As his tongue slowly weaved its way out of her, she dropped her hands from his head. She closed her eyes and took in deep and slow breaths. She felt him easing his way back up her. Her eyes opened and she stared at him. She only saw desire and nothing else.

He wrapped his hand around her neck and pulled her into a breathless kiss. His tongue circling around hers. He pulled from the kiss, bringing his mouth down to her flesh of her neck. She could barely keep up, as she was fighting exhaustion.

She closed her eyes and tried to focus on his intimate paths around her skin. Between kisses, she heard his words. "God, you're sexy!" She could relish in that forever. When she felt him retracting, she heaved a sigh. He fell off of her and she could hear the restlessness that he felt. "Wow..." he mumbled, as they both just laid there and tried to catch their breath. She closed her eyes and knew that this was going to complicate everything, but it was exactly what she needed to take her mind of everything that was going on.

***

Monday morning, Jeffrey walked into the office and as he passed Marisa's office, he couldn't even look up. When he had time to think, he realized that it wasn't right. He took advantage of the situation, of his venerability, and pushed it off to her.

He sat down at his desk, looking around the office. There were no signs of sex, but he held onto the visual memories and he couldn't get rid of them.

He looked down at his desk, where the picture that started everything was still lying in a heap of papers. He smelled her sweet perfume and instinctively kissed her, but it should have stopped at that.

He picked up the picture, clearly seeing Troy Houser as he watched his wife dance with the other man. There was a glare in his eyes and it wasn't able to be refuted. He had the strange feeling he did, similar to the one that he felt when Troy left their meeting.

As he was looking at the picture, he heard a knock on his door. He glanced up to see Marisa in his doorway. "I'm sorry to bother you, but can we talk?" She didn't give him a chance to answer her, as she entered his office and closed his door behind her. When she turned around, he tried to read her mind, yet he saw that it wouldn't be an easy task.

"What's on your mind?" He asked, putting the picture down and looking back up at her.

She was hesitant, glancing around his office and he wondered if she saw the visuals, too. "I want to talk about Saturday," she walked over and sat down in his chair.

He wanted to avoid it at all costs, but he could see that she was not having that in mind. "Okay."

"It wasn't planned..." she began.

"No...it wasn't," he concurred.

"I guess that I was wondering how you felt about it?"

He thought about that. He would be lying if he said that it wasn't what occupied every moment of his mind. He would be denying everything if he said that he didn't want to rip her clothes off and enjoy another day of sex with her.

He bit back the thought and just looked at her. "You are a very passionate woman, Jamison." He groaned, knowing what words he would speak next. "I'm not looking for a relationship."

"I'm not neither," she whispered.

"What we did on the floor of this office, needs to stay between us." She nodded, proving that she was aware of that. His eyes wandered to her lips, the same lips that he could have remained kissing all night, but he looked away.

"We let impulses take over and I'm too much of a stickler to make sure that never happens again."

Her face fell and she looked down at his desk. He knew that he saw hurt in her eyes, but she stood up and nodded. "I am glad that we're on the same page. It was something that we both needed in the moment, we claimed it, seized it, and that was it. Thank you for your time."

She turned from him and left his office. He hadn't expected her to be so casual about it, but he supposed he should have been glad. Instead, he was trying to figure out how he could forget it.

***

Marisa sank down in her chair, after leaving his office. She didn't know what she had expected him to say, but she didn't think he would resort to his abrupt attitude. As she was contemplating how to forget about him, her phone rang. She picked it up, "Hello?"

"Hey honey, I was just seeing how things were going?"

She groaned, hearing her mom's voice. She had given the phone number, because she didn't have her cell anymore.

Now she regretted it. "Things are going great. I absolutely love my job." She wanted to be as enthusiastic as she possibly could. She hadn't told her about the apartment, because she knew she would worry and that wasn't good for anyone involved.

"Good...good..." her mother was saying. "I was wondering if you had time to think about this weekend."

"I don't know mom. He has me working weekends and I might not be able to get away." She looked up and saw that he was entering her office, "I have to go. I'll try," she quickly hung up the phone and stood up. "I'm sorry, I..."

"Please, you don't have to apologize. Everything alright?" He asked, a look of concern etched on his face.

She smiled so show that everything was fine. "Yes, it's fine, but I did want to ask you something."

"Sure," he replied, taking a seat.

"Well, every Fourth of July my family has a big barbeque. The whole town comes and it's something pretty cool, but I haven't been back for it since I left home.

I was wondering if maybe you didn't need me this weekend and I could go back to Pennsylvania."

"Well..." he replied slowly, "you'll be in Ohio this weekend, for business."

Her eyes got big, "What?"

He pushed the folder toward her. "I forgot to mention that every year there's a two day lawyer's conference in Columbus Ohio. Your ticket and itinerary is inside."

She nodded, knowing that she couldn't change that. "Okay."

"I am sorry, Marisa," he spoke as he stood up. She saw that he appeared to be genuine.

"I understand," she replied, looking through the paperwork. She didn't see him as he left her office, but she pushed the folder away. She picked up the phone and called her mom back to give her the news. It couldn't be helped and she would just make her see that.

***

Jeffrey sat in another boring meeting. He didn't like coming to this conference, but it was necessary to keep face. As he was drowning out the topic at hand, about the quality of lawyer care, he glanced to Marisa, who was sitting next to him.

He wished things could have been different, but there was no way to go back. Every minute he spent with her, he grew more enamored with her beauty. Yet, it wasn't enough to make him throw out all worries and just let what happened...happen.

He shifted in his seat, to the growing erection in his pants. His leg slid along hers and she shot a look in his direction. "Sorry!" he whispered, turning his attention back to the speaker.

The speech lasted for another thirty minutes and when it was done and they were walking out of the room, he turned to her. "That...was interesting," she replied.

He laughed, "Well, you really don't have to lie."

She looked at him and they laughed together. She looked away and shrugged, "Yeah, it was pretty boring."

They headed out of the building and the warm air blew past him. "At least it was the last meeting for the day." He glanced at his watch and saw that it was five o'clock. "Want to grab a bite to eat before going back to the hotel?"

She paused. He saw her bite her lower lip. It was a trait he found endearing. "I don't know."

"Please, at least let me do that. It's the least I could do from dragging you to these boring meetings."

She slowly nodded, "Okay." She followed him to his car and he opened the door for her. She looked up at him and cocked her head. She shook her head and snickered, then got into the car.

He came around, but before starting the car he gave her an inquisitive look. "What's so funny?"

"I suppose that I am just thinking back to the first few days of working with you. You were anything but gentlemanly."

He nodded, thinking back to all the arrogance he portrayed. "I suppose I have changed...a little." He also knew that a big part of that was due to her.

"You have changed, but more than a little." She spoke, sitting back in her seat.

He started the rental and pulled from the parking lot. He saw her staring out the window, as if she was thinking. "Any preference of where to go?" He asked, breaking into the silence.

She shook her head, "Whatever!"

He continued to drive, until he was pulling into a Pizzeria. She opened the door, not giving him a chance to. He held back while she walked ahead of him. His eyes sauntered down her frame and then he cursed himself. This wasn't helping the fact that he didn't want to mix business with pleasure.

As he rushed to the door to open it up for her, their eyes met. Her smile was pure and sweet. She entered the restaurant and he knew that what he was doing to get her out of his mind wasn't working and it would require an adjustment...a big one.

***

Marisa tossed and turned in the bed. She didn't know what her problem was. It wasn't like she wasn't used to sleeping on a hard bed. She sat up in her bed and turned on the television. She flipped through the channels and landed on an old movie.

As she watched she began to imagine herself and Jeffrey portraying the characters. She groaned, when the leading male and leading female began kissing. It was like Jeffrey's hands were all over her body and his tongue was dipping into her mouth.

She quickly changed the channel. She didn't have time to have thoughts like that running through her mind.

She started watching a classic sitcom episode of *I Love Lucy*. She was laughing along with the television audience, when she heard the phone in her room ringing. She glanced at the clock to read eleven o'clock. She reached across the bed and answered the phone. "Hello?"

"Hello, Marisa...I'm sorry to call so late." There was a hesitation on his end. "Is that the television I hear?"

"Yeah, I couldn't sleep."

"Me neither," he admitted to her. "A lot on my mind."

"Right. There's been a lot of information thrown at you...I mean us, today. So, it makes sense that our minds are reeling."

There was a brief pause, before she heard him chuckling. "Yeah, that isn't exactly why I can't sleep." For a moment she wondered if it was because of her, but she didn't want to think foolish thoughts. "I actually am calling to tell you that the meetings for tomorrow have been cancelled. I just received an email, something about a water main break at the building they were using."

"Oh...that's too bad," she spoke, but she was really thrilled to know that they didn't have to sit through another boring meeting.

"Yeah, that's what I thought, too." He laughed, clearly seeing her sarcasm. "So, I was wondering...if you would want, that is...would you like to go visit your family tomorrow?"

Her jaw dropped. She processed his words, but wasn't sure if he truly meant them. "That's a three hour trip."

"I realize that. I actually know the Pittsburgh area well. Our plane doesn't leave until eight o'clock. We could get up early, you could visit them, and still be back in plenty of time to catch the plane to New York."

"You're going, too?" She asked, trying to catch her thoughts.

His light breathing was echoing through the phone. "I suppose that I could stay here and you could take the rental. I guess that I never really thought about that." She heard disappointment on his end. "Is that what you want?"

She shook her head, despite the fact that he couldn't see her. She knew that she wanted him to go, but she just was surprised to learn that he hand that in his mind. "You are more than welcome to meet me family."

"Well then...it's settled. Tomorrow we can get up at seven o'clock, get dressed, and head out. I'm sorry that you missed the barbeque."

"That's fine," she quickly spoke. She was still going to see her loved ones. "Thank you, Jeffrey."

"You are welcome." They disconnected the call and she hung up the phone. She began to reach for the phone again, but decided to leave it as a surprise and she knew that they would definitely be surprised.

***

They were about fifteen minutes from her house and Jeffrey began to question her about her family. He figured that he should have some idea of where she came from. "So, give me the lowdown about your family. How you grew up and what kind of upbringing did you have?"

She seemed to think about it and he noticed a slight hesitation before she replied. "Well, my mom used to be a nurse. Then she had me and decided that she needed to take some time off to raise me. She was going to go back when I was starting Kindergarten. However, she had my sister before getting that chance. She never went back." She looked out the window and he saw a smile on her lips. "She is a great Mom and I have truly been blessed."

"So, your sister...were you close?" He asked, generally interested.

She nodded, "She is my best friend." She then turned back to him and spoke, "How about you? Do you have any siblings?"

He shook his head; he wanted to have someone to grow up, with but he wasn't blessed like that. "Nope, only child."

She scrunched her nose, "You must have been spoiled."

He laughed, "You would be absolutely...wrong. I was given money when I needed it, but there was a lot I was lacking."

She showed signs of concern and empathy. "I know exactly what you mean."

He could see that she meant that and it felt good to find someone he could talk to. "Well, I know about your mom and your sister...tell me about your dad."

Her face turned grim and she faced the window. "We don't really talk about him." He could see that he struck an emotional chord. Yet, even though he saw pain in her eyes, she looked back at him and shrugged, "I suppose you might as well know. My dad is at the state prison. He was a drunk most of my life and would take it out on all of us. He left bruises on my sister and me for a good portion of our childhood."

He couldn't believe the truth that was coming out. He reached across the car and grabbed her hand. Their eyes met and he shook his head, "I am so sorry, Marisa. Any guy that does that to his kids and wife, deserves to be locked up."

He saw tears in her eyes as she nodded, "That's why I left right after graduation. I couldn't stand being in the same town with all the bad memories."

He squeezed her hand and her eyes wandered down to the hold. They remained holding hands while going the rest of the way. She pointed to several different streets to turn down, before they made their way to a cul-de-sac.

She pointed to a white house on the end and he pulled in front of the house. He reluctantly pulled his hand away as they got out of the car.

"Thank you!" she said, before they headed up the driveway. "This is exactly what I needed."

"It's my pleasure," he smiled, trying to ignore the fact that he would have given her the moon.

They headed up the steps and she knocked on the door. After a couple of minutes, an older woman opened the door. Her eyes got big and she covered her mouth. "Marisa?"

"Mom..." Marisa spoke. Her voice was shaky. Her mom opened the screen door and threw her arms around her. They held each other in an emotional embrace, while he stayed back. When they pulled away, she turned to Jeffrey. "Mom, this is Jeffrey Bradley...my boss."

Her mother turned to him, "Hello, sir."

"Please, call me Jeffrey." He replied, shaking her hand. "It's a pleasure to meet you."

She smiled, then turned back to her daughter. "I don't understand. I thought you said that you couldn't come this weekend." She held the door open, as they entered.

"I couldn't, but we had our meetings yesterday and they were cancelled for today. So, Jeffrey said that we could come here today." She was beaming and he was thankful that he had made the suggestion.

"Jeffrey, thank you so much."

He shrugged, "I am glad that I could make it work."

"Hillary is going to be so excited to see you." Her mother was saying. "Hillary...come down here."

"What is..." a voice from upstairs yelled. He looked up to see that Hillary was standing at the top of the stairs. "Marisa?" She ran down the stairs and jumped into her arms, they hugged for what felt like an eternity. "I...I don't understand." She pulled away and he saw that she was just as emotional. She glanced toward him and then back at Marisa. "Who is the guy?"

"This is my boss Jeffrey Bradley."

He shook her hand, "Hello, Hillary. Nice to meet you."

"Likewise," she smiled.

"Tell me everything that you have been up to," Hillary said, grabbing onto Marisa's arm and carrying her away into another room. He didn't know if he should follow or give them space.

"Would you like some coffee, Jeffrey?" Her mother asked him.

He smiled, "No thank you."

She nodded, "Make yourself at home," she then walked away. He awkwardly hung out in the foyer, leaning against the banister. He knew that Hillary and Marisa would want their space and he didn't want to be an intruder.

***

"Girl, you didn't tell me what a fine piece of specimen you were working for," Hillary spoke, as they took a seat on the couch.

Marisa rolled her eyes, "He's not bad."

"Not bad?" Hillary shook her head, "You are either blind or in denial."

Marisa knew that she definitely wasn't blind. She shrugged, trying to forget about it. "Tell me about you. Did I see something on your left hand?"

Hillary laughed, "If I would have known you were going to be here then I would have hidden it from you." She produced her hand and Marisa stared down at the shiny ring. "I'm engaged."

"Mom said you had news, but I had no idea."

"It just kind of happened. I met him two months ago when I was getting my car worked on. We instantly had a connection and then he asked me to marry him. We haven't even had sex...he wants to wait. Can you believe that?"

Marisa slowly shook her head, knowing that she was already one step ahead of that with Jeffrey. "I am happy for you."

"Thank you," she replied, staring down at her ring. Her eyes got big, "Maybe you could get one of these things if you make nice with the lawyer." She winked at her and Marisa playfully hit her on the arm. "Ouch," she laughed.

Marisa looked around the living room, "Speaking of...I wonder where he is."

"You know Mom. She's probably talking his ear off."

"I hope not," Marisa replied, feeling scared. She laughed, thinking of the things her mother could tell him about her.

She started to get up, but Hillary reached out for her hand, pulling her back down. She looked at her and she smiled. "He'll be fine. I want to hear everything that has been going on with you."

Marisa told her the things that she felt she could, conveniently leaving out the fact that she was technically homeless. About an hour later, her mother was calling them in the kitchen for lunch. They headed out of the living room, where she saw Jeffrey standing at the banister.

She caught his eyes and started to laugh. "What are you doing? You could have come in."

He smiled, "I figured you wanted some alone time. I thought about sitting out in the car."

She rolled her eyes, "Not necessary."

"I didn't know what deep secrets you were going to share and I thought if you wanted to talk about me...it would be easier while I wasn't around." He was smiling to show that he was teasing, but she blushed. She hoped that he didn't hear anything. "Did you?"

"Did I what?" she asked.

"Did you talk about me?" He asked with a wink.

She looked away from him, searching for what she could say to him, then decided that she would play along. "Wouldn't you like to know?" She winked, brushing past him and heading toward the kitchen. She was suddenly feeling pretty good about their relationship and wanted the easiness to continue.

***

Marisa didn't want the day to end. Her time with the family was going so well. She looked at Jeffrey as they were saying their goodbyes. He seemed to fit into the family and it was like they were a true couple. "Goodbye, Hillary." I hugged her tightly. "I'll be back soon."

She nodded, then turned to Jeffrey and shook his hand. "It was nice meeting you, Hillary." He then turned to her mother and shook her hand. "Thank you for being so hospitable."

"You are welcome back anytime."

He nodded, "I'll keep that in mind. Thank you." Marisa wondered if they would ever have another reason to bring him back to Pennsylvania.

"Goodbye, Mom," she hugged her mom. "I love you!"

"I love you, too." When she parted, she saw that there were tears in her eyes. She brushed away her own and then turned to Jeffrey.

They headed to the front door. He held the door open for her as she exited the house. She waved as they got to the car. Once inside, she felt the tears take over. She looked at him and he reached out and grabbed her hand. "Are you alright?" He asked.

She nodded, but she still felt the heaviness in her heart. "This meant a lot to me. You have no idea how much."

"I meant it, Marisa. I am glad I was able to do this." She turned back to the window and waved to them, as he pulled away. As the house faded from her view, she let out a sigh. "I better stop and get gas, before we get too far down the road. She silently nodded, as she leaned back in the seat and just let him drive. A few minutes later he was turning into a gas station. When he stopped the car, he turned to her. "Marissa..." he started.

"Yes?" she asked, giving him her attention.

"There's something I have been wanting to do." He leaned in and landed a kiss on her lips. His tongue swooped in, gently massaging her tongue. When he pulled away, she just stared at him. "Now, I'm going to get gas," he said, getting out of the car and leaving her there to think about his lips.

What the hell? She thought. She didn't know what it meant, only that her lips were on fire and her heart was racing. She watched him getting gas and he was looking away from the car. She shook her head, trying to regain her senses.

When he got back in the car, she didn't know if she should look at him or look away. She saw the smile on his lips, causing her to look at him. "What was that?" she asked, still stunned.

"What? I just wanted to do it. Is it a crime?"

She covered her eyes and slowly tried to forget the moment, but she couldn't. She didn't want a casual fling...a simple kiss here to just confuse her even more. She wanted the real thing and something that was lasting. "Don't do that again." She spoke, feeling a sense of nausea in her stomach.

"Marisa...I..." he began, but she didn't want to hear excuses.

"Jeffrey, don't do that again. Understand?"

He slowly nodded, "Loud and clear." He pulled out of the gas station and headed back to Columbus. She didn't care what he thought, but she was not going to be the person that screwed someone to get ahead in life. She deserved better than that.

***

Jeffrey had hoped things would lighten up between them on the airplane. However, he was left to kick himself for kissing her like that. He didn't mean for it to upset her the way that it did.

When she walked to her car in the airport parking lot, she didn't even allow him to walk with her. It was like nothing they had been through meant anything.

As he worked on Monday, he had hoped that she would need to talk to him about work stuff, but she never came to him. He had thought about calling her into his office and lying about needing her help with something, but he knew that would come across as wrong.

He left the office and found himself heading in the opposite direction of his car. He went into the bar to where he ordered a beer. He didn't drink much, but he knew that he needed something to take off the edge.

He slowly drank the beer and thought about the way the previous day ended. As he thought about it, he found his mind drifting to her scent, the way her body felt against his, the way her breath felt against his skin, and the way that he felt when he was with her. He took a drink of his beer and reached for his phone.

He searched for her cellphone number and then called it. It was a recording that came on. "We're sorry, the number you are trying to reach has been disconnected or changed." He disconnected the call and frowned, dialing it again and receiving the same message.

He put his phone away and took another drink, before throwing a tip of the tip jar and leaving the bar. He knew that he needed to tell her the truth, but he wouldn't be able to reach her if her number had changed. As he was walking back to his car, his eyes looked up and he saw Marisa and a man entering a hotel.

Her arm was linked through his and they were laughing. He paused, staring up at the hotel. It all made sense...Marisa was seeing someone else.

***

Marisa was getting good at avoiding him. She knew that the key was to not make eye contact and so far it was working. However, when she came back from lunch and found a note that there was a meeting with Troy Houser, she knew that that was coming to an end. At two o'clock, she headed to the boardroom. He looked up, as she entered. Then he looked back down at the notes.

"Am I just taking notes?" She asked, sitting down in a chair.

"That would be fine," he mumbled. It appeared that they were both avoiding each other. She flipped her notebook open to the page after her previous notes. "If you have anything to add, you can throw it in."

She gawked at him, unsure what to say. "Well, the last time we even really talked about this case was that night I showed you the picture. That was about a week ago. Any new developments?"

He shrugged, "Just wing it." The way he was being casual, surprised her. She couldn't believe she upset him that much.

She nodded, looking down at her notebook. When Troy walked into the room, she felt nervous. She tried to smile as he took a seat. "Mr. Houser, thank you for coming back in. We have a couple of questions. For starters, can you explain this?" He pushed the picture in front of Troy.

He looked at it and then looked up.

"Yeah, that's my ex and her boyfriend. That was taken while we were still married."

Marisa watched Jeffrey as he grabbed a marker and walked over to the picture, circling the spot where he was standing. "What about this?"

Troy looked down at the picture and his face turned red. "Uh..."

"You were spying on her yourself, you found her with this guy, and you became jealous. Is this all correct?"

"No..." he argued.

Jeffrey chuckled, then looked back his way. "You weren't jealous?"

"I was jealous, but this has nothing to do with why I'm here."

"Is that so?" Jeffrey asked, "The way I see it is you hired a PI. Then you realized that you didn't trust the PI's work, so you went on a hunt. You came across her and her lover at the same time that the PI did. You grew jealous, instantly filed for divorce and would have completely been satisfied with letting it go. However, you discovered that she was going to marry the guy she cheated on you with. So, that angered you and you vowed to do anything you could to make sure that she paid. How close am I?"

He looked between Marisa and Jeffrey. Marisa couldn't believe how much information he was throwing out there about Troy. "I am not on trial," he argued.

Marisa glanced at him, "Did she abuse the children?" She asked, softly. "Or, did you?"

She saw Jeffrey looking at her, but she didn't turn away from Troy's glare. "What?" He asked, but Marisa saw that he was not denying it.

Jeffrey turned to him, "Did you?"

Troy's mouth dropped open, but he did not deny the accusations. "I'm apparently going to need a lawyer." He spoke, looking at Jeffrey.

"You are and you won't find one here." He nodded, standing up and walking out of the office. Jeffrey reached for his phone and dialed a number. "Hey, Troy Houser is about to walk out of the building.

Detain him and call the cops. I'll be out in a minute." He disconnected the call. Jeffrey turned to Marisa, as she was standing up. She started to move past him, "How did you know?" He asked.

"I lived it, remember?" She shrugged, "It's all the same." She left the boardroom and headed back to her office. She closed her door and watched through the window as Jeffrey walked to the security station. She started to cry, feeling the pain from the years of abuse and knowing exactly what his kids had gone through.

***

Jeffrey waited until he knew that Marisa was leaving. He followed her out of the building and watched as she entered the hotel. He knew that it wasn't any of his business. If she was having sex with ten different men, he wouldn't be able to say anything. Although, that didn't stop him from heading to the hotel.

He entered cautiously and saw her get into the elevator. He watched as the numbers went up, stopping on floor three. He got in the other elevator and pushed the button to floor three. He prayed that when the door opened, he wasn't greeted by her. When the door opened, he peeked outside and saw her putting a key into the lock.

He held back, waiting for her to go in. He didn't know what he would say to her, but he knew that he was interested to confront her. He walked up to the door and knocked lightly. It wasn't long, before she was opening the door. She stared at him, "How did you know I would be here?"

"I saw you yesterday come into the hotel and today I followed you."

"Followed me?" She asked, anger taking over.

"I'm not proud of it, Marisa, but I was a little surprised. I know that I have no right to be jealous, but—"

"Jealous?" She asked, frowning.

"Yes...jealous. I know that I don't have any right to be jealous that you are having sex with someone else. I don't own any right to you. We aren't dating, but I do have strong feelings for you and I was going to tell you that yesterday if I could have gotten ahold of you.

Your phone has been disconnected and then I saw you with the guy yesterday...." He heard the sound of laughter, so he stopped talking. She was laughing so hard that she had to go back into the room and sink down on the bed. "What's so fun?"

"You're jealous..."

He rolled his eyes. He should have known that would be the only thing she would focus on. "Move past that and listen to the rest."

"You have it all wrong, Jeffrey. You have no idea just how much."

"Really, then explain it to me." The words came out brash and he regretted that.

Her face turned red and she stood up from the bed. "I don't owe you an explanation. Like you said...I can sleep with anyone I want." She crossed her arms, as if to wager him.

"I know you can." He glanced around the room, noticing the boxes lying around the room.

He looked at her. "I shouldn't have come." He stepped back, as her eyes wandered down to the boxes and then looked back at him.

"Aren't you going to question the boxes?"

"You don't have to tell me anything," he said, reaching for the door.

"Jeffrey, you didn't get ahold of my cellphone, because I cancelled it. The guy you saw is my best friend, Chad. He's been the only friend that I have had and that has supported me." He felt a pang of guilt hit him.

"Those boxes are here because I have been living here. I was evicted from my apartment exactly a week after I got this job."

"Marisa, I had no idea." He spoke, thinking back to when she asked for an advance and he shot her down. "Why didn't you tell me?"

"Pride, stupidity, because I didn't want to play the sympathy card."

"You should have told me," he spoke, softly.

She nodded, "In hindsight...maybe I should have, but it's over and done with and hopefully in a couple of weeks I will be back on my feet...thanks to you and your job."

His hand fell from the door handle and he moved closer to her. "I'm sorry that you have had to go through this."

She moved in closer to him, "It hasn't all been bad."

He brushed her hair behind her shoulder and moved in closer to her, bringing his lips to hers. He would move slowly, if she would just give him the chance. He parted from the kiss and rested his head against hers, "I'm sorry Marisa that I just wasn't honest with you," he whispered, feeling her breath against his skin.

"I have strong feelings for you, too," she admitted. She closed her eyes, as they stood with their heads together and his hands caressing her neck. "Make love to me," she spoke, opening her eyes.

He hadn't thought she would speak the words, but he slowly began to remove her clothes. Her hands went to his outfit and she was removing them from his body. He flicked her bra off with his wrist and then lowered her panties, while she grabbed onto his boxers and pulled them to the ground.

His hand wrapped around her neck and passionately held onto a kiss. She parted from the kiss, to push him down to the bed. Once he was lying on the bed, she straddled him. He slowly entered her, as her lips went down to his. Her body bounced up and down his manhood as her tongue dove inside his mouth.

His hands massaged her large breasts, while their tantalizing kiss took over. She gyrated her hips against his, moving him in and out of her. He pulled from the kiss, because of the intensity of his gyrations. "Ugh...ugh...oh God...ugh..." he moaned, moving his arm around her body and pulling her down to his thrusts. "Ahhhhh..." he cried, as he reached orgasm.

"Ugh...ugh..." she moaned, moving on top of him with comfort. Her gentle whimpering was breathlessly encompassing him. She crashed down on top of him, as he slowly retracted from her. They kissed, while she wrapped her arm around him.

He was relieved that everything was working out and that all the confusion was gone, because he had no doubt in his mind that they would spend many days and nights exploring the possibilities and he was excited for it to begin.

****

The Billionaire's Caregiver

People often think a new beginning is something that happens when there is a tragedy. Shelby Watson, on the other hand, disagrees entirely. Sometimes, a new beginning can simply happen to someone, and not be some epiphany out of the ashes of what was once a mess.

Simply put, life happens, but starting over is never easy. Shelby sighed and stretched out her legs on the sofa. Tomorrow, she would start again. Never one to be defeated, she knew she could pull herself out of this "new mess" she was in.

There was something about the way her big toe poked through the worn socks that made her rethink that idea entirely.

"You and me, Dobbs...she scooped up her puppy who had buried its head under the thick blanket. "All we really need is each other." Dobbs was a Chihuahua mix. Shelby found him by the door of her apartment one day, and when she opened her apartment door, he ran right in, in front of her.

He had been there since. It may have been the forlorn look he had about him that Shelby found endearing, or just the fact that he was standing there soaked to the bone. Whatever it was, Shelby knew she couldn't leave him out there, so let him stay.

The sound of banging caused Shelby to wince slightly. The pipes in this old building were always making some awful noise whenever someone was taking a shower. Shelby looked around at her efficiency apartment.

Clean and tidy it, was her home. She lived in the 3rd block of town. The lower the number indicated the worse sections of town. This was no exception. Her neighbors all consisted of drug dealers and prostitutes, though none unfriendly. Shelby would work early mornings and try to be home before dark. As long as she kept to herself nothing bad would happen to her...well less likely to, anyway.

All of the details of her life had changed now. The part-time morning job she had been able to find, she had lost. Nothing of her doing, simply a cut in positions at the senior home she was working at. They had pulled her aside that morning and given her the bad news.

"Shelby, your work here has always been wonderful. I hope you realize this is not a reflection on the quality of your work. It's simply based on the financial needs of the company." Dr. Brenner sighed and looked over at her as he delivered the news.

"Many of the seniors are moving into better equipped facilities and they...well they already have staff there. He ran his thin bony fingers through is even thinner hair.

It was obvious to Shelby this wasn't something he enjoyed doing and decided to help take the pressure off.

"I understand Dr. Brenner. I really do. I just don't know how I'm going to make it now." Life had always been a series of ups and downs for Shelby, and this was just one more set back. She stood to stand and extended her hand to Dr. Brenner.

"Thank you for helping me get things going here Dr. Brenner. The last three years have been wonderful. I hope you will let me use you for a reference." He stood and methodically pumped her hand, covering the hands with his other one.

"I really am sorry, Shelby."

There was a sense of helplessness that Shelby felt when she headed home. Now, she and her pup gracefully sat on the old worn sofa she had gotten from the thrift store down the street. Shelby decided it was time to start sorting the factors of her life out. She jumped up and grabbed her notebook from the counter.

Determined, she created her spreadsheet, lists of bills, things to do, what not to do, etc. Balancing her checkbook, Shelby calculated that she was ok for the next three weeks, but when the rent was due, she would be in trouble. She walked into her kitchen and pulled some canned spaghetti from the cupboard, methodically putting them in a bowl and then the microwave.

This is not where she envisioned herself a few years ago. She had big plans to go back to college to get her graduate degree in nursing. She was barely scraping by, but she knew that her resilience was powerful and that she would make it through. The one thing she was sure of was that she would not cry about it but would just keep moving on.

The next day things seemed bleak. Shelby walked to the corner store and bought a newspaper and began sifting through the want ads looking for a job. She wasn't above doing anything and would do whatever necessary to keep things going. Sitting on her foot, she took notice of anything related to her field first.

Under the dark header she saw an ad for a home health nurse. Perfect. She picked up the phone and called, but was greeted by a nasty voice.

"Kayla I told you I can't do this with you right now. You will just have to trust me. It's better this way." Shelby winced at the explosion.

"I'm sorry Sir. I think I may have the wrong number, I was calling about an ad." As she began to cradle the phone back into the receiver, she heard him yell.

"Wait yes, Oh God I'm an idiot. Miss...Miss?" He was obviously flustered.

"I'm here."

"Good. I'm terribly sorry. Your number was just like someone else's, and well... Ok, so yes, can you come out today? I need to wrap this up before I leave this weekend, and I have only gotten a few responses."

Encouraged, Shelby shot up out of her chair. "Yes, of course I can, what time?"

"Um, let me think." She heard shuffling on the other end. "How about now?"

"Now?" Shelby looked around mentally, figuring out what to wear." Sure now is good. I just need an address."

After getting all the necessary information, Shelby changed into a light grey dress and black boots. Shelby pulled her hair back and gathered up all of her references. As she started to walk out, she grabbed her purse and said a silent prayer.

"Wish me luck Dobbs, this is for dinner tonight."

Maneuvering her car down the highway was easy. Shelby loved road trips and had been into the town of Fauquier many times. Often considered the "rich" area, she never had much opportunity or reason to come this far out before.

Today was different. She had an interview, and hoped it would fix this mess she was in. Pulling down the long winding road into the countryside, Shelby admired the houses as she passed them. Most of them were old, and laced with gingerbread latticework. They looked warm and cozy. At the end of one street in particular, Shelby found the house she was looking for.

All she could do was stop the car and look up in awe. There is no way, she thought to herself. The magnificent mansion was on top of a ridge high above the roadway. There was a winding back entrance that was gated, and the front lawn was landscaped perfectly. Shelby glanced over at her car with it's rusted out fenders, and wondered if she really knew what she was doing.

With a sigh, she pushed her glasses back up and drove up the driveway. She pulled off to one side, straightening her dress as she stood and shut the door. She mentally prepared herself for whatever was on the other side of the door, took a deep breath, and knocked.

Billionaire, Michael had never been more frustrated in his life. He was handling the merger of two companies, trying to line up a meeting with his partner, and simultaneously trying to find someone who could come sit with his grandmother. At 40, Michael was all business with dark hair and eyes and didn't have time for anything frivolous. His grandmother was his only soft spot. She had raised him, and her encouragement is what created the man he was now.

Suddenly ill, the doctors believed she had a stroke, and now she was in bed and unwilling to do anything. He glanced over at the clock. Where was this girl anyway? She seemed interested, but was probably another "no show." He started gathering up some paperwork just as there was a knock at the door.

Shelby waited patiently. When the door finally did open, she found herself stunned for a moment as she looked at the most handsome man she had ever met. Tall and dark, he was almost like a sculpture. Trying not to stare, she attempted to recover quickly.

"Hello, I'm Shelby. We spoke on the phone." She held out her hand to him.

Michael took her hand, shaking it lightly. He was not without his own reaction to her. Small and petite, she had hair piled on top of her head. It was dark brown and a wonderful accent to her almond-colored eyes. She wore little makeup, and was a natural beauty.

"I'm glad you're here, though I thought you would have been here sooner." Shelby frowned at the gruffness in his voice. He wasn't as pleasant as she had hoped.

"I'm sorry, I was coming from Manassas." She tried not to take offense, as he was obviously very busy.

"I see. I am looking for someone to care for my grandmother. Full-time and an occasional Saturday. I try to be here on weekends as often as I can, and she has another nurse as well. I need someone who can try to get her to do more, or at least want to. She had a stroke a month ago and the doctors think she should be fine to get out again, but she is simply laying there." He paused to look her over.

"You're very small. Are you sure this is something you'd be interested in?"

Shelby felt the anger rise. "Mr. Jameson, I can assure you that I am very capable, despite your opinion of my small stature. Would it be possible for me to meet your grandmother? I think it's always important to see how well I click with someone."

"Sure that's fine. She knows you're coming. We can head upstairs in just a few moments. I'd like to ask a few more questions first, if that's ok?"

"Certainly." Shelby relaxed slightly. The fact that this guy was an ass made the fact that he was gorgeous much easier to look past.

"Ok so I see you are working with Everest Healthcare. Do you plan to continue to do that as well?"

"If so, this may be a bad idea. I really need 100% attention for this. My grandmother is very important to me, and multitasking is something most people think they are good at, but sadly..." he looked her over once again, "are not."

Fuming, Shelby responded in clipped tones. "No, I am no longer there. I was let go recently." Before she could elaborate, Michael interjected quickly.

"Why? Was there some sort of horseplay or something? I won't tolerate any of that at all, Miss Watson. I simply won't. You do seem rather young, and I can understand if this is something that you don't feel you can handle."

He stood up as if he was dismissing her entirely.

Panic set in but even that wasn't enough to calm her anger. "Mr. Jameson, I have been working at this for a long time. I am not young, as you so nicely put it, and as a matter of fact, I'm 33. I love this type of work, and the reason I was let go was for budget cuts, not horseplay. Perhaps if you allowed people to answer your questions without simply writing them off, you would have more candidates for this position."

Shelby stood to leave.

Fire and ice. That was all he could think of. She was absolutely adorable when she was mad. He could see how her nose slightly turned red as she had been giving him a piece of her mind and although not used to being talked to like that, he gained a new kind of respect for her.

"Point taken, Miss Watson. Shall we go meet my grandmother?" He held the door to the hallway for her and allowed her to pass as he made his way up the stairs motioning for her to follow. Shelby was surprised she had even gotten this far. He was a real piece of work, this guy. Money did that to people, she thought, and could only assume that was it. Along the hallway there was artwork. Some bright, some dull, and some muted. It was a lot to take in. As they rounded the top of the stairs, Shelby looked down and couldn't help but think that her meager apartment would fit in the foyer below.

Nancy Jameson was in good spirits. She wanted to do more, but her body just wouldn't allow her to. Besides, when she is here like this, Michael comes around more. He was her only grandson and always had been her favorite.

She had three granddaughters, but they all had their own families, and were too busy to ever visit. Michael had always been special. He had dark coloring like his grandfather and was just as stubborn. She smiled warmly as Michael entered the room with a petite brunette in tow.

Nancy didn't miss the sparks that flew from the young lady's eyes as Michael made some comment on how he could show her how to use the elevator if need be.

"Grandmother this is ...I'm sorry what your name was again?" He did look guilty so Shelby took pity on him and extended her hand to Nancy.

"Hello my name is Shelby, how are you?"

"Well I'm in this bed deary so not very good, I suppose." She winked at Shelby and smiled wide.

"My grandson feels like he needs to find someone to watch over me and make me do things I am not ready to do. I suppose that's why you're here my dear. Come over here and let me get a look at you."

Having taken an immediate liking to Grandmother Nancy, Shelby complied and walked over towards the bed. Nancy noticed how her grandson followed Shelby's every move. This was interesting indeed and was exactly the distraction she needed!

After a while of discussion and rules, Shelby stood to leave. "It was very nice to meet you Miss Jameson."

"Now Dear, if you're going to be here with me all the time, I insist you call me Nancy or Grandmother, whatever suits you."

"Grandmother, no one has offered Miss Watson a job yet. I hardly think she needs to start calling you Grandmother." Michael chuckled.

"Michael Dear, it is my money is it not?" Grandmother smiled up at him lovingly and patted his hand on the bed. "So, I say she is hired."

"Shelby that is if you will take the job of course."

Never a person to have nothing to say, it took everything Shelby had not to laugh at the interplay. It would seem that Grandmother Nancy was the only one to bring Michael down a peg or two. If for that reason alone, Shelby would take the job.

"I would love to Nancy." Shelby smiled up at Nancy and then at Michael.

There was some mix of being irritated by his grandmother's words and being floored by the smile that Shelby gave him. He didn't know what to say. After clearing his throat, he kissed his grandmother on the head and turned to leave.

"Miss Watson, if you will kindly follow me back down stairs, we can go over pay and hours, and so on."

Shelby said her goodbyes again and followed Michael down the stairs. He even smelled good, like leather and soap. What was most adorable was the way his hair curled in the back of his neck just slightly. What in the world was wrong with her?

Never suckered in by the connection between men and women, she usually had a fairly good grasp on self-control. Sure she had met a few nice guys and done her share of dating, but that was a long time ago and there had been no one in at least three years. Maybe that was it, she needed to get out more.

Offering her a chair, Michael detailed the terms and pay of the job. More money than she could imagine, Shelby sat stunned while he rambled on.

"Miss Watson is that acceptable?" She glanced up at him sharply. Oh no, what had she missed.

"Yes of course, that's more than fair."

"When can you start?" He watched her closely. He could almost watch the play of emotions she was thinking and feeling.

"Anytime is fine. I don't live far, even if I was late today. So I am free anytime."

"I'm not sure if you realize that this job is more than just being here from one time to another. Obviously, you will have to move in here, as that is part of the deal." He moved to gather up his things and glanced at his watch. He was already late and was starting to get irritated, as this matter should have been handled over an hour ago.

"Oh no, I can't do that Mr. Jameson, I have my own place. I'll stay there." He was surprised. He had seen the worn shoes she was wearing, and heard the racket her poor car made as it climbed the hill to the house. He just assumed that she would be more than happy to move in.

"Suit yourself, but I may need you sleep over on occasion. Is that fair?" He caught her eye again and reached out to shake her hand.

He was all business and it suited him. She reached out and felt the warmth as he took her hand in his. She felt like he lingered perhaps just a second longer than normal; but it was probably just her imagination. There was something powerful about the way he carried himself. Like right now, just staring at her. Closing her eyes for a moment, she managed to get out "Of course."

After saying their goodbyes, Shelby made her way to the car and headed home. What was it about Michael Jameson that made her crazy? He was arrogant, stubborn and bossy. He was also handsome, loving to his grandmother, and made her feel safe. All of that from one visit. Thankfully, he didn't live in the house year round, or she would be in trouble for sure.

The next few months were a flurry of activity. Shelby commuted every day to her job with Nancy which she loved, and had enough money to pay up her rent for a while. Michael and she spoke on the phone almost every day discussing Grandmother's day and how things were going. He typically had a joke to tell, but on some days, he was distant and moody.

Either way, they had come a long way and she considered him a friend. Gone was the canned spaghetti, and Shelby was actually able to cook food for herself. Even Dobbs was happier. She had just settled down to watch TV for a bit before turning in when the phone rang. It was a frantic Michael.

"Watson, my grandmother seems to have had a heart situation of some kind. I am in town and headed to the hospital and she has asked to see you." He was obviously in pain as he choked it out. Despite their differences, Michael had been nothing but nice with her and she didn't want to see him hurt. Worry was a motivator for Shelby and she immediately started to change clothes as he talked.

"..wanted to know if she had been acting differently lately or anything?"

"NO no she's been fine, and we have actually been walking a few times and..."

He cut her off immediately. "You had her walking? What in the world, Watson were you thinking? She wasn't ready for that. Just come to the hospital as soon as you can." He hung up leaving Shelby stunned.

She was frustrated herself wondering if he was right. She gathered up her purse and headed downstairs. Trying to avoid the people in the halls, she made it to her car safely and let out a deep sigh. Unfortunately, it was not meant to be. As she turned the key nothing happened. Slowly, she laid her head on the steering wheel. What now? She jumped out to look under the hood. Apparently, sometime during the night, someone had stolen her battery... now she was stuck. Knowing she could never forgive herself if she didn't see Nancy, Shelby made her way back to her apartment and called him.

"Yes What!" He yelled into the phone.

"Michael, please don't yell at me."

"Oh it's you. I'm sorry, Watson. The number thing again. Yes what's up?"

After much explaining, it was settled that Michael would come by and pick Shelby up on his way. She wasn't too far from the hospital herself but at night it was better to ride with someone. A few minutes later Shelby heard the knock on her door and opened it to a disheveled Michael. He was a mess, worry etched on his face, but handsome as ever.

Michael took in the apartment, if that's what you call it. Small but tidy, he imagined she could do just about everything. His issue was with her neighbors.

"This..is where you live, Shelby?" He gestured to the occupants sitting in the halls and the loud music.

"Yes why?" Shelby had her pride. This was her place and it wouldn't sit well if he was insulting.

"I'm terrified for my safety out there. I can't imagine how you've made it all this time. You're so small and there are at least 20 people just hanging outside."

"I am not so small and I am just fine. Let's go." She crammed her gloves into her purse and yanked open the door leaving it open so he could follow.

In the car Michael looked over at her. She had her signature bun in place and there was a pained look on her face. Obviously, he had hurt her feelings.

"Look Watson, I'm sorry. I didn't mean anything by it. I just worry. I mean grandmother worries about you is all." She had noticed the slip he made and smiled inwardly. He cared.

They arrived at the hospital and Nancy looked tired, but was noticeably happy to see her two favorite people. These two sure move slowly and I'm not getting any younger, she thought. She smiled at them both. What a striking couple they make. This little heart "issue" was just what was needed to bring them together for a while.

"Oh my dears, I'm so happy to see you both. They say I'm ok but are keeping me for a few days for observation. Can you imagine two whole days? I'll be bored out of my mind." Truthfully, she was glad. She had been feeling uncomfortable today but she knew Michael was coming to town and wanted he and Shelby to spend some time together.

"I'm just glad you're ok." Shelby was concerned at how pale she was. "This is my fault. We shouldn't have been walking this week."

"Oh pish posh. It's probably just gas or something." Michael rolled his eyes at his grandmother.

It was at that time that the nurse came in.

"I'm sorry, but you'll both have to get going Mrs. Jameson need to rest..."

They said their goodbyes and headed out front. Michael was very quiet, brooding again over some business merger gone wrong or something. She glanced over at him and he was caught up in thought, so she let the ride continue on in silence.

They pulled into her apartment complex and Shelby began to open the door.

"Wait, Watson I'm going up with you. I need to make sure you get in there in one piece."

"You don't have to do that Michael, I'm fine." She started walking and he followed anyway.

As they reached the top stairs of the building, a man reached over and touched Shelby on her leg making her jump. Michael immediately jumped.

"Don't touch her!" he moved between Shelby and the man.

"Michael it's fine. He is harmless." Secretly, she was touched that he jumped to her rescue.

Opening the door, they went inside. Michael was again impressed by the simple charm of her place. He sat down on the sofa and was greeted by a flying ball of fur. "Oh my, what is this?" He scruffed the dog on the back of the head and it bounced off.

"You once told me you had a dog but I hardly think that little thing qualifies, Watson." He smiled up at her.

Shelby had moved to the other end of the couch. "He is something, that's for sure." She giggled as they watched him get into a fight with a dog toy.

"You should just move into the house with us, Shelby." Hearing these words, Shelby caught her breath. She even noticed he had used her first name.

"Why would I do that? I'm perfectly fine here." What she didn't say was that she couldn't handle watching him with the various women he dated. She cared too much about Grandmother Nancy to ruin her relationship by being too close to him."

At that moment there was an obvious gunshot. Michael jumped up, and in his demanding voice she had grown to love he simply stated, "Get some things, Watson you're going with me."

The ride to the house was uneventful. Shelby knew he was mad, but to be honest, she wasn't sure why. He parked his car in front of the house and they went inside together. "You can have the room down here. I'll sleep upstairs and you know your way around. I'm getting a drink, I certainly need it."

She could use one herself, she thought as she went into the spare room downstairs. Changing into pajamas, letting her hair down, and tucking Dobbs into the bed, Shelby decided to go into the den where Michael was and get that drink. If, for any other reason but to calm her nerves. Knowing they were here alone was setting her on edge.

He was sitting in the leather-bound chair by the fireplace. He already had a drink, or was it two? Nothing could prepare him for her entrance. It felt like someone had punched him in the stomach. She was in all pink and her hair was flowing down her back. This casual image of her was one he had played out in his mind during one of their conversations on the phone. He had thought about it ...and now here it was.

He watched her walk over to the bar, pour a drink for herself, and tip it back. Impressive he thought. He stood up and moved closer to her. He could see all the shades of auburn in her hair when he was up close like this, she smelled like honeysuckle.

"You're moving in here, Watson." He said it with a finality that only made her angry.

"You can't tell me what to do, Michael. I work for you, but you don't own me." She was flushed with anger as he turned towards her.

"You could be killed, Watson. That place is dangerous, men groping you in the halls and gunshot...real actual gunshot, Watson." He ran his hand though his hair.

"My grandmother would kill me if anything happened to you and I didn't try and stop it." She couldn't help but feel some disappointment at the words. She had hoped he would say something about how he cared.

"I'm not moving in Michael. Let it go." She put her glass down and turned to leave. He grabbed her left arm and spun her around. It could have been the alcohol or the stress of the day, but something made him lose himself in that moment.

He gripped her wrist tighter than he meant to and put his right hand into the waves of her hair, pulling her towards him. The kiss had meant to be angry. He needed her to listen to reason but what started out hard, became softer, deeper, and more meaningful. Slowly, he dropped her other wrist and cupped her face in his hands, nipping at her lips and taking in the smell of her skin. When the kiss broke, he looked up at her.

"Watson, you're driving me crazy." He dropped his hands back down and watched the emotions play out on her face. Rocked to her core, Shelby could only stand and wait. Wait for the fluttering to subside, wait for her heart to stop racing, and wait for him to stop looking at her so intently. Not knowing what to say, she turned and walked stiffly back into her room. He followed her.

"Talk to me Watson. Why are you running from me? I know you feel this craziness just like I do."

"Yes I do Michael and that's why I won't live here." She turned to look at him. "I am a mess inside and I need you to go and leave me be so I can think straight." She saw the pained look on his face but heard him leave the room.

Shelby laid in bed thinking about that kiss. His kiss only intensified the connection they had. It wasn't all her. That was comforting, but what wasn't, was that she couldn't stop the fluttering she felt deep down. The way he moved towards her and the way he kissed deeply and without thought.

Laying here was obviously not going to figure it all out. She decided to go get a drink of water. They came from such different worlds. He always had someone worldly on his arm, some debutante. She had even met a few of them when he was there and she had been working.

The one thing they all had in common was that they were beautiful. Always regal and gorgeous, she always found something to do to keep away from them. After they would leave, Grandmother Nancy always had some snide comment about each one that made Shelby giggle.

"He will never find the right one unless he shops from a different field," she would say. Smiling now, Shelby opened the refrigerator door and started sifting through things until she found exactly what she wanted. Cake, it was the best cake around and had been left over from a party Grandmother Nancy had earlier that week. She stood there eating quietly, not hearing him until he spoke.

"You have quite the "strictly business" thing going on here, Watson."

She slammed the door shut on impulse, having been caught red handed.

"Yeah I try." She smiled slightly. He walked over to her and with one finger, wiped the chocolate off her bottom lip.

Feeling the heat begin to creep up again, Shelby took a step back.

"We need to talk Watson, and now." He walked until she had backed up to the bar. He moved his face closer to hers.

"I think it's obvious that I want you. I don't know how else to put it." The bluntness of the statement made Shelby gasp.

"The only way I'm going to stop trying is if you tell me you don't feel the same way." She was pinned between him and the bar and he was watching her face.

"Michael let me go," she tried to squirm but it was no use. She was stuck.

"Just tell me you don't want me to touch you and I'll leave you alone Watson. Just say it."

Knowing full well she felt the same way he did she, Shelby did the only thing she thought was right. She looked up at him and ran her finger down the right side of his face.

"I can't tell you any of that, Michael because I want the same thing." Before she could finish the words, he crushed his mouth to hers. He put his hands in her hair tilting her head back more. She kissed him back more fervently, having let go now. He lifted her up off the floor and put her on the bar top. Running his hands along her legs, all the while teasing and nipping her bottom lip.

"We should stop Michael." It was more of a pant than a statement.

"You're right, Watson, we should, but I can't. Not anymore." Pulling her to him, he lifted and carried her into the bedroom and kicked the door shut behind him. Sitting her down, she stood motionless, watching him take his shirt off and move towards her. She was frozen to the spot she stood on, not knowing what to do next.

He walked to her and started slowly unbuttoning the front of her pajamas. Each button exposed new skin that he had to kiss. He loved the way she smelled of sunshine and honeysuckle. He looked up at her.

Needing no words, she walked backwards towards the bed, pulling him with her as they went. Sliding back onto the comforter, he followed, pressing the length of him against her body. He looked down and knew in that moment, he was lost. Her hair spilled across the pillow, her lips were parted slightly from being thoroughly kissed, and her eyes were shining up at him. He could tell she was scared and excited. He ran his finger along her bottom lip.

"I need to hear you say it, Shelby. I need us to be real in this moment and together."

He gazed at her. "I can stop if you want, but you need to tell me now before I can't anymore." His honestly made her want him even more. She slowly pulled her shirt off and tossed it to the floor.

"I want you Michael, I always have." Needing no further encouragement, Michael stood and took off the rest of his clothes looking down. He stood back for a moment, letting himself take in her naked form. She was perfect.

Once, he thought her tiny, but looking at her now, he could see every curve she was given. Almost scared to touch her, she made the move first.

"I'm getting a little self-conscious Michael. What's wrong with me?" She started to cover up again.

"No don't "...he grabbed her hand. "You're beautiful, Watson, absolutely beautiful." He laid down on the bed again, taking a moment to calm his racing heart. He was acting like a teenage school boy, wondering why in the world was so nervous.

This was different. He knew it and probably always had, but he needed her to feel loved, wanted, and cherished.

The night progressed, and the two made love into the early hours of dawn. Before falling asleep, the last thing she heard was him saying her name and draping one arm across her body. Sometime during the night, Shelby got cold, having been woken up by something, only to find herself naked as the day she was born. She tried to keep from moving, but right before she almost fell asleep, she felt Michael's arm grasp her stomach and pull her into him. He kissed her ear and they drifted back to sleep for a few more hours.

Never a late sleeper, Michael woke up to greet the day with a smile on his face. Shelby was amazing. She was not just beautiful, she was the type of woman men dream of. She gave as much as she received, and never held back. This was something Michael couldn't help but admire. He looked at her lying among the sheets as he headed upstairs to shower and get ready for the day. He just didn't have the heart to wake her up.

Shelby woke up to the smells of coffee and the clink of pans. She rolled over to snuggle in more and her eyes flew open as she remembered...everything. Oh wow she had never been so careless in her life. She scrambled to jump in the shower before he found her. Before she was soaped up she heard him come into the bathroom.

"Watson, I see you're joining me today finally." He chuckled.

"Michael really, I am in the shower, I'll be right out." She could only smile as she heard him hum a tune as he left.

What would she do now? It had happened and there was no going back, but she could stop it now. Now that they had gotten it out of their system, she could put Michael Jameson out of her mind altogether.

She entered the kitchen, dressed for the day and ready to go to the hospital. Michael was cheery and leaned towards her as if to get a kiss. She managed to avoid it discretely.

Frowning, Michael went back to cooking. Something was wrong. Breakfast passed with no mishaps and they set off for the hospital.

Grandmother was overjoyed to see them. They each took a side and listened to her tell them about how awful the night had been and the bed situation. She moved on to complain about the food and how happy she would be at home. She could tell something was amiss between the couple, but it would sort itself out.

Michael was having a hard time understanding what Shelby was thinking. The night had been something people only dream about and yet when he got close to her, she ran. Something wasn't right, but he would find out soon enough.

The doctors came in and discussed the grandmother's situation. They equated it to a chemical reaction to something she ate, at which grandmother smiled. They passed the morning laughing with her, planning the next event. At lunch, the doctors ordered them out, saying she needed her rest, so the couple decided to go to a nearby restaurant for something to eat.

It was a beautiful café, overlooking a pond and situated amongst lush landscaping. They dined on wine and oysters, which were new to Shelby. Michael was about to broach the subject plaguing him, when a woman came up to the table.

"Michael darling, where have you been?" The woman was like something from the cover of a magazine. She had on long flowing pants and a silk shirt complete with a huge brimmed hat.

"Baby, I have missed you so much. How nice of you to bring the maid to lunch." She smiled over at Shelby, who immediately excused herself and went outside.

Angry Michael pushed the woman back away from him. "I told you to leave me alone. Why are you here? Stop calling me and stop following me."

Without waiting for an answer, he stormed out onto the street and to his car. Shelby was standing by the passenger side and he opened the door, then went to his side and got in.

"I'm sorry, Watson that was ...the number..." at her confused look he added "remember when you would call and I thought it was her?"

"Aha that is her." Shelby still felt awful about the exchange and self-conscious as well. The maid, really?

When they arrived at the house, Shelby went to her room. Thinking she would have some time to think, she was surprised when Michael stormed in behind her.

"What the hell Shelby, after last night I thought,"

"What...you thought we would just act like nothing happened? You think I would go away? Well I'm not. I love Grandmother Nancy and I'm not going anywhere."

"What are you talking about Shelby? I don't want you to go anywhere. I want you here. With me." He said it with such finality, Shelby could do no more than look up at him.

"What?"

"I love you Shelby. I have since the day we met and you came here. But when I was at your place and heard that gunshot it was all I could do to not kidnap you myself and tie you up here so I could keep you safe."

"But I'm not like you Michael. She called me "the maid" for goodness sake." She looked down for a moment.

"Shelby do you really think I care one moment about what people think?" I want you and I choose you."

Tears were flowing freely now as Shelby looked up at him.

"Well," He asked impatiently.

"Well what? " She was confused.

"Damn it Shelby, you're killing me. Do you or do you not feel anything for me?"

Laughing, she ran into his arms and kissed him. "Michael I have loved you from the moment you opened that door."

He let out an audible sigh. Happy and content, he pulled her close to him and kissed her deeply.

Hand in hand they headed back to the hospital. Grandmother had taken a nap and was refreshed as she looked out the windows to the parking lot. Seeing Michael, she smiled. He really was a good boy. But what made her happiest was seeing him hand in hand with Shelby.

Perhaps her plan had worked after all, and if she played it just right, she could somehow start planning a Fall wedding at the house. She may be getting old, but this was enough to keep her busy for at least a good many years to come.

****

About the Author

J.L. Ryan is a bestselling romance author who loves writing billionaire romance, bad boy romance, BBW romance, slow burn romance, angsty romance, and second chance romance books. She's been an author for the past 20 years, and has conducted literary workshops to help aspiring authors improve their writing skills. She likes to attend author and publishing conventions, workshops, and seminars, where many of her books are featured. Here are some of the many genres, categories, and characters she enjoys writing about: Billionaire Romance Bad Boy Romance Plus Size Romance A Good Billionaire Love Story Or Series Playboy Romance Wealthy Romance Hot Romance Novels Steamy Romance Novels Second Chance Romance Alpha Male Romance Older Man Younger Woman Romance Billionaire Obsession Billionaire Bachelors Rich Romance Rich Man Poor Woman HEA HEA Romance Small Town Romance Return To Hometown Romance Slow Burn Romance Angsty Romance Boss Romance Office Romance Lawyer Romance Medical Romance Bad Boy Alphas

Billionaire Bad Boy Romance Bad Boy Rebels Sweet Romance Inspirational Romance Clean And Wholesome Romance Contemporary Romance Contemporary Women's Fiction And More...